THE PELICAN SHAKESPEARE

GENERAL EDITOR ALFRED HARBAGE

AS YOU LIKE IT

WILLIAM SHAKESPEARE

AS YOU LIKE IT

EDITED BY RALPH M. SARGENT

PENGUIN BOOKS

PENGUIN BOOKS
Published by the Penguin Group
Viking Penguin Inc., 40 West 23rd Street,
New York, New York 10010, U.S.A.
Penguin Books Ltd, 27 Wrights Lane,
London W8 5TZ, England
Penguin Books Australia Ltd,
Ringwood, Victoria, Australia
Penguin Books Canada Ltd, 2801 John Street,
Markham, Ontario, Canada L3R 1B4
Penguin Books (N.Z.) Ltd, 182–190 Wairau Road,
Auckland 10, New Zealand

Penguin Books Ltd, Registered Offices:
Harmondsworth, Middlesex, England

First published in *The Pelican Shakespeare* 1959
This revised edition first published 1970
Reprinted 1972, 1974, 1976, 1978, 1979, 1980, 1981,
1983 (twice), 1985 (twice), 1986, 1987, 1988

Library of Congress catalog card number: 71-98355
ISBN 0 14 0714.17 0

Printed in the United States of America by
Kingsport Press, Inc., Kingsport, Tennessee
Set in Monotype Ehrhardt

CONTENTS

PUBLISHER'S NOTE

Soon after the thirty-eight volumes forming *The Pelican Shakespeare* had been published, they were brought together in *The Complete Pelican Shakespeare*. The editorial revisions and new textual features are explained in detail in the General Editor's Preface to the one-volume edition. They have all been incorporated in the present volume. The following should be mentioned in particular:

The lines are not numbered in arbitrary units. Instead all lines are numbered which contain a word, phrase, or allusion explained in the glossarial notes. In the occasional instances where there is a long stretch of unannotated text, certain lines are numbered in italics to serve the conventional reference purpose.

The intrusive and often inaccurate place-headings inserted by early editors are omitted (as is becoming standard practise), but for the convenience of those who miss them, an indication of locale now appears as first item in the annotation of each scene.

In the interest of both elegance and utility, each speech-prefix is set in a separate line when the speaker's lines are in verse, except when these words form the second half of a pentameter line. Thus the verse form of the speech is kept visually intact, and turned-over lines are avoided. What is printed as verse and what is printed as prose has, in general, the authority of the original texts. Departures from the original texts in this regard have only the authority of editorial tradition and the judgment of the Pelican editors; and, in a few instances, are admittedly arbitrary.

SHAKESPEARE AND
HIS STAGE

William Shakespeare was christened in Holy Trinity
Church, Stratford-upon-Avon, April 26, 1564. His birth
is traditionally assigned to April 23. He was the eldest of
four boys and two girls who survived infancy in the family
of John Shakespeare, glover and trader of Henley Street,
and his wife Mary Arden, daughter of a small landowner
of Wilmcote. In 1568 John was elected Bailiff (equivalent
to Mayor) of Stratford, having already filled the minor
municipal offices. The town maintained for the sons of the
burgesses a free school, taught by a university graduate
and offering preparation in Latin sufficient for university
entrance; its early registers are lost, but there can be little
doubt that Shakespeare received the formal part of his
education in this school.

On November 27, 1582, a license was issued for the
marriage of William Shakespeare (aged eighteen) and Ann
Hathaway (aged twenty-six), and on May 26, 1583, their
child Susanna was christened in Holy Trinity Church.
The inference that the marriage was forced upon the youth
is natural but not inevitable; betrothal was legally binding
at the time, and was sometimes regarded as conferring
conjugal rights. Two additional children of the marriage,
the twins Hamnet and Judith, were christened on Feb-
ruary 2, 1585. Meanwhile the prosperity of the elder
Shakespeares had declined, and William was impelled to
seek a career outside Stratford.

The tradition that he spent some time as a country

teacher is old but unverifiable. Because of the absence of records his early twenties are called the "lost years," and only one thing about them is certain – that at least some of these years were spent in winning a place in the acting profession. He may have begun as a provincial trouper, but by 1592 he was established in London and prominent enough to be attacked. In a pamphlet of that year, *Groats-worth of Wit*, the ailing Robert Greene complained of the neglect which university writers like himself had suffered from actors, one of whom was daring to set up as a playwright:

... an vpstart Crow, beautified with our feathers, that with his *Tygers hart wrapt in a Players hyde*, supposes he is as well able to bombast out a blanke verse as the best of you: and beeing an absolute *Iohannes fac totum*, is in his owne conceit the onely Shake-scene in a countrey.

The pun on his name, and the parody of his line "O tiger's heart wrapped in a woman's hide" (*3 Henry VI*), pointed clearly to Shakespeare. Some of his admirers protested, and Henry Chettle, the editor of Greene's pamphlet, saw fit to apologize:

... I am as sory as if the originall fault had beene my fault, because my selfe haue seene his demeanor no lesse ciuill than he excelent in the qualitie he professes: Besides, diuers of worship haue reported his vprightnes of dealing, which argues his honesty, and his facetious grace in writting, that approoues his Art. (Prefatory epistle, *Kind-Harts Dreame*)

The plague closed the London theatres for many months in 1592–94, denying the actors their livelihood. To this period belong Shakespeare's two narrative poems, *Venus and Adonis* and *The Rape of Lucrece*, both dedicated to the Earl of Southampton. No doubt the poet was rewarded with a gift of money as usual in such cases, but he did no further dedicating and we have no reliable information on whether Southampton, or anyone else, became his regular patron. His sonnets, first mentioned in 1598 and published without his consent in 1609, are intimate without being explicitly autobiographical. They seem to commemorate the poet's friendship with an idealized youth, rivalry with a more favored poet, and love affair with a dark mistress; and his bitterness when the mistress betrays him in conjunction with the friend; but it is difficult to decide precisely what the "story" is, impossible to decide whether it is fictional or true. The true distinction of the sonnets, at least of those not purely conventional, rests in the universality of the thoughts and moods they express, and in their poignancy and beauty.

In 1594 was formed the theatrical company known until 1603 as the Lord Chamberlain's men, thereafter as the King's men. Its original membership included, besides Shakespeare, the beloved clown Will Kempe and the famous actor Richard Burbage. The company acted in various London theatres and even toured the provinces, but it is chiefly associated in our minds with the Globe Theatre built on the south bank of the Thames in 1599. Shakespeare was an actor and joint owner of this company (and its Globe) through the remainder of his creative years. His plays, written at the average rate of two a year, together with Burbage's acting won it its place of leadership among the London companies.

Individual plays began to appear in print, in editions both honest and piratical, and the publishers became increasingly aware of the value of Shakespeare's name on the title pages. As early as 1598 he was hailed as the leading English dramatist in the *Palladis Tamia* of Francis Meres:

As *Plautus* and *Seneca* are accounted the best for Comedy and Tragedy among the Latines, so *Shakespeare* among the English is the most excellent in both kinds for the stage: for Comedy, witnes his *Gentlemen of Verona*, his *Errors*, his *Loue labors lost*, his *Loue labours wonne* [at one time in print but no longer extant, at least under this title], his *Midsummers night dream*, & his *Merchant of Venice*; for Tragedy, his *Richard the 2*, *Richard the 3*, *Henry the 4*, *King Iohn*, *Titus Andronicus*, and his *Romeo and Iuliet*.

The note is valuable both in indicating Shakespeare's prestige and in helping us to establish a chronology. In the second half of his writing career, history plays gave place to the great tragedies; and farces and light comedies gave place to the problem plays and symbolic romances. In 1623, seven years after his death, his former fellow-actors, John Heminge and Henry Condell, cooperated with a group of London printers in bringing out his plays in collected form. The volume is generally known as the First Folio.

Shakespeare had never severed his relations with Stratford. His wife and children may sometimes have shared his London lodgings, but their home was Stratford. His son Hamnet was buried there in 1596, and his daughters Susanna and Judith were married there in 1607 and 1616 respectively. (His father, for whom he had secured a coat of arms and thus the privilege of writing himself gentleman, died in 1601, his mother in 1608.) His considerable earnings in London, as actor-sharer, part owner of the Globe, and playwright, were invested chiefly in Stratford property. In 1597 he purchased for £60 New Place, one of the two most imposing residences in the town. A number of other business transactions, as well as minor episodes in his career, have left documentary records. By 1611 he was in a position to retire, and he seems gradually to have withdrawn from theatrical activity in order to live in Stratford. In March, 1616, he made a will, leaving token bequests to Burbage, Heminge, and Condell, but the bulk of his estate to his family. The most famous feature of the will, the bequest of the second-best bed to his wife, reveals nothing about Shakespeare's marriage; the quaintness of the provision seems commonplace to those familiar with ancient testaments. Shakespeare died April 23, 1616, and was buried in the Stratford church where he had been christened. Within seven years a monument was erected to his memory on the north wall of the chancel. Its portrait bust and the Droeshout engraving on the title page of the First Folio provide the only likenesses with an established claim to authenticity. The best verbal vignette was written by his rival Ben Jonson, the more impressive for being imbedded in a context mainly critical:

... I loved the man, and doe honour his memory (on this side idolatry) as much as any. Hee was indeed honest, and of an open and free nature: had an excellent Phantsie, brave notions, and gentle expressions.... (*Timber or Discoveries*, ca. 1623–30)

*

The reader of Shakespeare's plays is aided by a general knowledge of the way in which they were staged. The King's men acquired a roofed and artificially lighted theatre only toward the close of Shakespeare's career, and then only for winter use. Nearly all his plays were designed for performance in such structures as the Globe – a three-tiered amphitheatre with a large rectangular platform extending to the center of its yard. The plays were staged by daylight, by large casts brilliantly costumed, but with only a minimum of properties, without scenery, and quite possibly without intermissions. There was a rear stage gallery for action "above," and a curtained rear recess for "discoveries" and other special effects, but by far the major portion of any play was enacted upon the projecting platform, with episode following episode in swift succession, and with shifts of time and place signaled the audience only by the momentary clearing of the stage between the episodes. Information about the identity of the characters and, when necessary, about the time and place of the action was incorporated in the dialogue. No place-headings have been inserted in the present editions; these are apt to obscure the original fluidity of structure, with the emphasis upon action and speech rather than scenic background. (Indications of place are supplied in the footnotes.) The acting, including that of the youthful apprentices to the profession who performed the parts of women, was highly skillful, with a premium placed upon grace of gesture and beauty of diction. The audiences, a cross section of the general public, commonly numbered a thousand, sometimes more than two thousand. Judged by the type of plays they applauded, these audiences were not only large but also perceptive.

THE TEXTS OF THE PLAYS

About half of Shakespeare's plays appeared in print for the first time in the folio volume of 1623. The others had been published individually, usually in quarto volumes, during his lifetime or in the six years following his death. The copy used by the printers of the quartos varied greatly in merit, sometimes representing Shakespeare's true text, sometimes only a debased version of that text. The copy used by the printers of the folio also varied in merit, but was chosen with care. Since it consisted of the best available manuscripts, or the more acceptable quartos (although frequently in editions other than the first), or of quartos corrected by reference to manuscripts, we have good or reasonably good texts of most of the thirty-seven plays.

In the present series, the plays have been newly edited from quarto or folio texts, depending, when a choice offered, upon which is now regarded by bibliographical specialists as the more authoritative. The ideal has been to reproduce the chosen texts with as few alterations as possible, beyond occasional relineation, expansion of abbreviations, and modernization of punctuation and spelling. Emendation is held to a minimum, and such material as has been added, in the way of stage directions and lines supplied by an alternative text, has been enclosed in square brackets.

None of the plays printed in Shakespeare's lifetime were divided into acts and scenes, and the inference is that the author's own manuscripts were not so divided. In the folio collection, some of the plays remained undivided, some were divided into acts, and some were divided into acts and scenes. During the eighteenth century all of the plays were divided into acts and scenes, and in the Cambridge edition of the mid-nineteenth century, from which the influential Globe text derived, this division was more or less regularized and the lines were numbered. Many useful works of reference employ the act–scene–line apparatus thus established.

Since this act–scene division is obviously convenient, but is of very dubious authority so far as Shakespeare's own structural principles are concerned, or the original manner of staging his plays, a problem is presented to modern editors. In the present series the act–scene division is retained marginally, and may be viewed as a reference aid like the line numbering. A star marks the points of division when these points have been determined by a cleared stage indicating a shift of time and place in the action of the play, or when no harm results from the editorial assumption that there is such a shift. However, at those points where the established division is clearly misleading – that is, where continuous action has been split up into separate "scenes" – the star is omitted and the distortion corrected. This mechanical expedient seemed the best means of combining utility and accuracy.

THE GENERAL EDITOR

INTRODUCTION

As You Like It assembles a mixed cast of distinct individuals, insulates them temporarily in a pleasantly habitable woodland, and allows them to devote themselves to the pursuit of happiness. In the case of several characters the pursuit takes the form of ardent and successful courtship. To many readers, audiences, and producers, an escape into the Forest of Arden for a brief season with Rosalind and Orlando, Jaques and Touchstone, seems happiness enough.

Those who look to comedy for amusement, laughter, a play of the mind, here also find Shakespeare's plenty. His Arden contains people whose ideas on the pursuit and even the nature of happiness prove widely diverse. Vague as the boundaries of the forest may be, they are confining enough to produce frequent and intimate contacts between these people as they go about their separate pursuits. Sometimes their meetings provide amusement simply by the inherent incongruity of the situation, as when Touchstone, the born urbanite, becomes entangled with Audrey, the country wench, each impelled by different motives. At other times, the characters themselves take advantage of the situation to heighten the amusement, as when Rosalind in disguise draws out Orlando on the subject of his love, or seizes her unexpected opportunity to lecture Phebe and Silvius. Occasionally in these meetings, particularly those involving Touchstone, Rosalind, or Jaques, the dialogue becomes wittily brilliant.

Shakespeare's light touch allows an audience or reader to skim over the intellectual edge of such passages. They are frequently capable, however, of producing a double-take.

In such juxtapositions the characters are led to sharpen up their individual ideas on the world and the way to happiness in it. These views not only reveal the character of the persons who express them, but illustrate widely different ways of seeing the world and conducting oneself in it. Each view springs from position in life, from character, and from personal experience, and is recognizable and viable (at least in the comedy); but when set beside a different reading of experience, each criticizes the other, each is seen to be partial. Yet they do not cancel each other out. The comic process, the civilizing procedure, requires the audience to hold all views in mind in the complicated overview that is the humane achievement of comedy.

The conflicting opinions in Arden tend to center around two aspects of the pursuit of happiness: the effect of surroundings, natural and social, and the nature and role of love and marriage. Since most of the characters are city dwellers, temporarily exiled to the country, they canvass pretty thoroughly the merits of a country atmosphere as an aid to happiness. The Duke Senior prefers a healthy country to a corrupt city; he admires the rugged features of country living as conducive to sane thinking; yet most of all he would like a healthy court-urban life. Touchstone, on the other hand, undisturbed by such moral discriminations, dislikes the country because it lacks creature comforts and sufficient cultural level to appreciate his wit. The Duke's retainers, scarcely noticing the lack of urban amenities, happily revert to the lives of their feudal forebears, and enjoy the forest life in hunting, eating, and singing. "I would not change it," says Amiens. Jaques, who seeks pleasure perversely in the achievement of melancholy, discovers in Arden ample occasion to exercise his sour talents, but he thinks it folly to live there. Finally, the genuine countryman finds the shepherd's life a source of happiness in its independence and security: "Sir, I am a true laborer; I earn that I eat, get that I wear, owe no man hate, envy no man's happiness."

Likewise the role of love and marriage provides a theme with variations. With worldly realism Touchstone views marriage as the answer to desire; his future wife sees it as a way to social improvement. Jaques regards love as a silly weakness. Silvius and Phebe take love as the whole of life, and make of it a painful frustration. Orlando and Rosalind are the romantic lovers, yet they know they have to live in a world busy with other occupations and preoccupations. Their problem is to domesticate love (a kind of madness) in marriage. In subjecting love to the corrosives of mundane attitudes, they do not destroy romantic love, but place it firmly in the real world.

Those who stay to look into the play a little longer may find another level to Shakespeare's vision. Perceptive readers and audiences become aware of the undertone of genuine melancholy which sounds through the major characters. The Duke and his fellow exiles have sufficient reason for this melancholy: they have faced a corrupt power, been victimized for their very virtues, and unjustly driven from public society. Shakespeare paints this corrupt authority with care. It forms, in fact, a major pole of contrasts to the life in Arden. Those who have faced corruption have been sickened by it; but given a forest island of temporary escape they have begun to reconstruct their lives and society. The natural woodland provides a morally restorative and regenerative stimulus (an idea which Shakespeare developed further in *The Winter's Tale*). Instead of sinking into despair Hamlet-like, here with the astringent qualities of forest life that "feelingly persuade me what I am," the Duke Senior has been able to "translate the stubbornness of fortune / Into so quiet and so sweet a style." In like manner, Orlando and Rosalind have achieved their happiness by being able to keep their spirits high and their minds alert to the realities of the world. The play thus presents the view that human beings, given a brief respite from corruption and placed in the healthy environment of nature, can and will build a good life. In entitling his play *As You Like It*, Shakespeare seems to express his confidence that we, his audience, share his vision.

It has been said that comedy makes the facts fit the dream. *As You Like It* presents a Shakespearean fusion of the visionary and the realistic. Shakespeare submits the dream to the facts; what happens is that the dream gives meaning to the facts – the stubborn actualities, infused with meaning, make the vision real.

Through the apparently casual flow of events in *As You Like It* may be seen some of Shakespeare's most skilled dramatic structure. In the first act he presents his sound characters as victims of a hostile world, and reveals the mutual love between Orlando and Rosalind. When in the second act he brings his characters to the salubrious environment of Arden he does not divert attention to a possible clash between the good forces and the bad; nor does he arouse any doubt as to the possible outcome of the principal love affair. In short, he eschews melodrama. Rather, Shakespeare concentrates on the present situation of the characters in the forest and their formation of a new community. In bringing these characters together in "encounters" he is not bothered by improbabilities: that two persons in love banished from different places on separate occasions should turn up at the same place, that the forest should contain both "literary" shepherds and genuine shepherds, that vengeful pursuers should be quickly converted to a new life on arrival in the forest. His care is directed to bringing the right persons together at the desired time. Thus, just before the first forest meeting between Orlando and Rosalind, Orlando confronts and overcomes Jaques; just before the second meeting, Rosalind encounters and defeats Jaques. Immediately after she has presented Orlando with false views of love in order to test him, Rosalind meets Phebe and gets a chance to express her genuine convictions. In the progress of the play the sequence of encounters forms a virtual permutation of character confrontations, a structural feature pleasing in itself. But through this sequence, with its cumulative revelation of characters, attitudes, relationships, and conflicts, Shakespeare presents that manifold view and acceptance of diversity within pattern which makes *As You Like It* a paradigm of civilized society.

Francis Meres does not include *As You Like It* in his list of Shakespeare's plays (*Palladis Tamia*, 1598). On August 4, 1600, the Lord Chamberlain's Men entered in the Stationers' Register "As you like yt, a booke" as one of four plays "to be staied" (i.e. to be held from publication). The play can thus be dated as of 1599 or early 1600.

Shakespeare's comedy is based on the prose romance *Rosalynde, Euphues' Golden Legacie* (1590) by Thomas Lodge, which had in its turn been suggested by the pseudo-Chaucerian *Tale of Gamelyn*. Shakespeare elaborates the role of Rosalind, somewhat curtails that of Orlando, and develops the character of the banished Duke from his slight role in *Rosalynde*. Jaques, Touchstone, and Audrey are wholly Shakespeare's creations. Although he presents most of the incidents in the story, he is careful to remove the bloody battle between the forces of the two dukes, and to substitute for it the conversion and retirement of the usurping duke.

Rosalynde exhibits the highly wrought style, with its balanced opposites and moral illustrations, made popular by John Lyly in *Euphues, The Anatomy of Wit* (1578). Thus Lodge writes: "Infortunate Rosalynde, whose misfortunes are more than thy years, and whose passions are greater than thy patience! The blossoms of thy youth are mixed with the frosts of envy, and the hope of thy ensuing fruits perish in the bud." In the midst of the colloquial prose which he uses for most of his drama, Shakespeare allows Touchstone to parody such Euphuism. Shakespeare's amusement at the expense of his source does not stop with a travesty of its style. Using the pastoral framework of *Rosalynde*, *As You Like It* ridicules the artificiality of the pastoral conceptions so popular in the poetry, fiction, and drama of his day. The introduction of genuine shepherds into Arden gives the literary figures, Silvius and Phebe, an anemic appearance. Further, Shakespeare makes Phebe something less than captivating in beauty, Silvius something less than manly in his abasement. Pastoral literature based its appeal on the fantasy that city people, by retiring to a shepherd's life, could escape the pressures of social responsibility, to concentrate on the fulfillment of personal desires. In Silvius and Phebe, Shakespeare shows that love, when divorced from the rest of life, becomes a tyrant in itself. By contrast, Rosalind and Orlando recognize that love must be taken as a part of social reality. *As You Like It*, while actively exploiting some of the appeal of pastoral escapism, contains within itself a critique of its conventions.

As You Like It also provides amusement at the expense of the elements of affectation in the current fashion for melancholy. The pretensions of the melancholy man to superiority are ridiculed when Jaques, impressed by Touchstone's cynicism and envious of his license, is moved to exclaim, in unconscious irony: "O that I were a fool!" Shakespeare even pinpoints his satire by making Jaques a melancholy traveller, a type of refined affectation. "A traveller!" declares Rosalind. "By my faith, you have great reason to be sad. I fear you have sold your own lands to see other men's. . . . And your experience makes you sad . . . and to travel for it too." As opposed to such loutish comic figures as Launce and Bottom in earlier plays, Touchstone represents the first of Shakespeare's witty professional court jesters. With his carnal eye and clever tongue, Touchstone provides amusement and a critical underview of human relations; yet he too, like Jaques, is revealed as the victim of his own folly.

To balance, as it were, the high proportion of prose in *As You Like It*, Shakespeare introduces the largest number of lyrics in any of his plays. They become an essential part of the atmosphere of Arden. The most famous of these, "It was a lover and his lass," sung by two page boys, was arranged as a two-part madrigal by Thomas Morley and published in his *First Booke of Ayres* (1600). The date suggests that Morley's may well have been the music for the original performance. Except for those sung by Hymen, the other songs are given to Amiens, evidently played by an adult actor-singer. (The earliest known surviving settings for "Blow, blow, thou winter wind" and "Under the greenwood tree" are those by Dr T. A. Arne, 1740.) It is now generally assumed that the part of Touchstone was originally played by Robert Armin, who replaced Will Kempe in the Lord Chamberlain's company some time about the turn of the century. In his *Notes* (1774) the scholar Edward Capell recorded, as a story current in Stratford, that a relative of Shakespeare remembered him as an actor in the part of an old man carried on the back of another. This story, amplified in other eighteenth-century accounts, forms the basis of the pleasant but tenuous tradition that Shakespeare was the original actor of the part of Adam.

The comedy was not revived in the Restoration period, but "improved" versions were acted in the eighteenth century. With the nineteenth century, and the Romantic approach to Shakespeare, *As You Like It* took on new popularity. To-day it holds a steady place in the active repertory of the Shakespearean theatre. Surveys regularly record at least half a dozen productions a year. With its many outdoor scenes the play has long been favored for open-air performances.

Among the many characters in *As You Like It*, two at least possess the depth and fullness to make them memorable: Jaques and Rosalind. Jaques, in his effort to establish himself as the superior person, stands outside life and merely observes it; he refuses to become committed, engaged. From this vantage point he shoots his criticism. Thus he can sum up the Seven Ages of Man in a series of vignettes, sharp in visual and auditory imagery – but constituting a view which leaves human life without meaning. (Jaques, in fact, uses the same metaphor, representing the same attitude, as Macbeth's "a poor player / That struts and frets his hour upon the stage," spoken when life has lost its meaning for Macbeth.) Shakespeare immediately counters Jaques' view by introducing Orlando carrying old Adam; these two reveal mutual devotion and love, the inward qualities which make all the difference in life. But they require commitment. Jaques, in the effort to avoid commitment, has become a traveller. In his role as outside observer, he never truly experiences life, either within himself or in relation to those around him. Dimly aware of his own emptiness, he cherishes his melancholy not only as a critical view of the world but as the sole achievement of his travels. His attitude, like that of Touchstone, presents a subtle inhibition to all meaningful action. The Duke Senior, Orlando, and Rosalind must all combat it, each in his own way. When Jaques reveals his single impulse to action, to scourge the world with satire, the Duke rises in anger. A man who sees only bad in the world, in fact has given himself up to it, cannot know the good: such a reformer will only destroy the good, by spreading corruption. At the end, Jaques, unsatisfied with the full life he has just witnessed in Arden, goes off once more looking for something to fill his own inner hollowness.

Rosalind, on the other hand, has had almost too much involvement with the world. She has encountered so many briers that she has to struggle with genuine melancholy. Rosalind has committed herself, engaged her heart; in so doing she has increased her own vulnerability; but she leads a full inner life, where she experiences silent pain –

and also intense delight. Rosalind keeps herself alert to the world around her, to its snares and its opportunities. Outwardly she displays gaiety and wit with firmness and generosity. Inwardly she recognizes love as a kind of romantic madness, yet the very force that gives warmth and meaning to life. In her determination to maintain love in the midst of workaday pressures, she has the daring to submit her lover, in advance, to the worst that can be said and thought of love domesticated in marriage. In the test, and its successful outcome, we know that she will continue to make life engaging and rich, for herself and those around her. It has often been suggested that women are the great civilizing force. Shakespeare in his portrait of Rosalind has come close to showing us why.

Although the play ends in the traditional battery of marriages, we may notice as evidence of Shakespeare's direction in comedy that all the exiled characters who have gone through their period of reformation in the forest will not stay in it but are now to return to court, there to play their renewed part in civilized life. As Jaques says to the restored Duke:

> You to your former honor I bequeath;
> Your patience and your virtue well deserves it.

Haverford College   Ralph M. Sargent

NOTE ON THE TEXT

As You Like It was first printed in the folio of 1623, from what textual scholars now believe to have been a theatrical prompt-book or a transcript of one. The act–scene division of the folio is supplied marginally in the present edition, and all material departures from the folio text are listed below except for extensive relineation. A number of prose passages, notably II, vi, 1–16; III, iv, 1–13; IV, iii, 1–5; V, ii, 13–18, are set as verse in the folio.

The adopted readings in italics, most of which first appeared in the later folios or in eighteenth-century editions, are followed by the folio readings in roman.

I, i, 40 *Ay* I (thus throughout)   102 *she* hee

I, ii, 50 *and* (omitted in F)   54 *Touchstone* Clowne (thus throughout)   85 *Le Beau* the Beu   95 *decree* decrees   232 *lifeless* liuelesse

I, iii, 74 *her* per

II, i, 49 *much* must   59 *of the country* of country

II, iii, 10 *some* seeme   16 *Orlando* (omitted in F)   58 *meed* (some copies of F read 'neede')   73 *seventeen* seauentie

II, iv, 39 *O Phebe, Phebe, Phebe!* (separate line in F)   40 *thy wound* they would   64 *you,* your

II, v, 38–39 (F reads 'Here shall he see, &c.')   43 *Jaques* Amy (designation continues through l. 51)   50 *An* And (thus throughout)

II, vii, 38 *brain* braiue   55 *Within* (omitted in F)   64 *sin* fin   87 *comes* come   182 *Then* the   198 *master* masters

III, ii, 11 *Master* Mr (thus throughout)   25 *good* pood   139 *her* his   152 *How now? Back, friends.* How now backe friends: 226 *such* forth   232 *thy* the   234 *heart* hart   245 *b' wi'* buy   342 *deifying* defying

III, v, 104 *erewhile* yerewhile

IV, i, 1 *be* (omitted in F)   26 *travel* travaile   28 *b' wi'* buy   44 *heart-whole* heart hole   194 *in, it* in, in

IV, ii, 12 *(The rest shall bear this burden.)* (F prints as part of song)

IV, iii, 5 s.d. *Enter Silvius* (follows l. 3 in F)   143 *In* I

V, i, 36 *sir* sit   54 *policy* police

V, ii, 7 *her* (omitted in F)   30 *overcame* overcome   59 *heart* hart

V, iii, 18 *ringtime* rang time   29–32 *And . . . springtime, &c.* (follows l. 20 in F)   39 *b' wi'* buy

V, iv, 34 s.d. *Enter . . . Audrey* (follows l. 33 in F)   77 *to the* ro   108 *her* his   126 *heart . . . heart* hart . . . hart   158 *them* him   165 *were* vvete

AS YOU LIKE IT

Duke Senior, in banishment
Duke Frederick, his brother and usurper
Amiens } *lords attending on Duke Senior*
Jaques
Oliver, eldest son of Sir Rowland de Boys
Jaques } *younger sons of Sir Rowland de Boys*
Orlando
Le Beau, a courtier attending on Duke Frederick
Charles, a wrestler at the court
Adam, an old servant to Sir Rowland de Boys
Dennis, a servant to Oliver
Touchstone, a clown
Sir Oliver Mar-text, a country curate
Corin } *shepherds*
Silvius
William, a country fellow
Hymen, god of marriage
Rosalind, daughter of Duke Senior
Celia, daughter of Duke Frederick
Phebe, a shepherdess
Audrey, a country wench
Lords, Pages, and Attendants

Scene : *Oliver's orchard ; Duke Frederick's court ;*
the Forest of Arden]

Enter Orlando and Adam.   I, i

ORLANDO As I remember, Adam, it was upon this fashion
bequeathed me by will but poor a thousand crowns, and, 2
as thou say'st, charged my brother on his blessing to
breed me well : and there begins my sadness. My brother
Jaques he keeps at school, and report speaks goldenly of
his profit. For my part, he keeps me rustically at home 6
or, to speak more properly, stays me here at home un- 7
kept : for call you that keeping for a gentleman of my
birth that differs not from the stalling of an ox ? His
horses are bred better, for, besides that they are fair with
their feeding, they are taught their manage, and to that 11
end riders dearly hired ; but I, his brother, gain nothing
under him but growth, for the which his animals on his
dunghills are as much bound to him as I. Besides this
nothing that he so plentifully gives me, the something
that nature gave me his countenance seems to take from 16
me : he lets me feed with his hinds, bars me the place of a 17
brother, and, as much as in him lies, mines my gentility 18
with my education. This is it, Adam, that grieves me ;
and the spirit of my father, which I think is within me,
begins to mutiny against this servitude. I will no longer
endure it, though yet I know no wise remedy how to
avoid it.

I, i The orchard of Oliver's manor house   **2** *but poor* merely   **6** *profit*
progress; *keeps* maintains   **7** *stays* detains   **11** *manage* actions and paces
16 *countenance* attitude   **17** *hinds* farm hands   **18** *mines* undermines

Enter Oliver.

ADAM Yonder comes my master, your brother.

ORLANDO Go apart, Adam, and thou shalt hear how he will shake me up.

26 OLIVER Now, sir, what make you here?

ORLANDO Nothing. I am not taught to make anything.

OLIVER What mar you then, sir?

29 ORLANDO Marry, sir, I am helping you to mar that which God made, a poor unworthy brother of yours, with idleness.

32 OLIVER Marry, sir, be better employed, and be naught awhile.

34 ORLANDO Shall I keep your hogs and eat husks with them? What prodigal portion have I spent that I should come to such penury?

OLIVER Know you where you are, sir?

38 ORLANDO O, sir, very well: here in your orchard.

OLIVER Know you before whom, sir?

ORLANDO Ay, better than him I am before knows me. I
41 know you are my eldest brother, and in the gentle con-
42 dition of blood you should so know me. The courtesy of nations allows you my better in that you are the first born, but the same tradition takes not away my blood were there twenty brothers betwixt us. I have as much of my father in me as you, albeit I confess your coming
47 before me is nearer to his reverence.

OLIVER What, boy!
        [Strikes him.]

ORLANDO Come, come, elder brother, you are too young in this.
        [Seizes him.]

26 *make* do (but Orlando pretends to take it in another sense) 29 *Marry* why, indeed (originally an oath by the Virgin Mary) 32–33 *be naught awhile* i.e. go to the devil 34–35 *eat husks . . . prodigal portion* (alluding to the Prodigal Son, who wasted his patrimony and then had to eat with the swine; see Luke xv, 11–32) 38 *orchard* garden 41–42 *gentle . . . blood* bond of family loyalty 42–43 *courtesy of nations* recognized custom (of primogeniture) 47 *reverence* revered rank

OLIVER Wilt thou lay hands on me, villain?

ORLANDO I am no villain. I am the youngest son of Sir 52
Rowland de Boys; he was my father, and he is thrice a
villain that says such a father begot villains. Wert thou
not my brother, I would not take this hand from thy
throat till this other had pulled out thy tongue for saying
so. Thou hast railed on thyself. 57

ADAM Sweet masters, be patient: for your father's re-
membrance, be at accord.

OLIVER Let me go, I say.

ORLANDO I will not till I please. You shall hear me. My
father charged you in his will to give me good education:
you have trained me like a peasant, obscuring and hiding
from me all gentlemanlike qualities. The spirit of my 64
father grows strong in me, and I will no longer endure
it: therefore allow me such exercises as may become a
gentleman, or give me the poor allottery my father left 67
me by testament; with that I will go buy my fortunes.
[Releases him.]

OLIVER And what wilt thou do? beg when that is spent?
Well, sir, get you in. I will not long be troubled with
you. You shall have some part of your will. I pray you
leave me.

ORLANDO I will no further offend you than becomes me
for my good.

OLIVER Get you with him, you old dog.

ADAM Is 'old dog' my reward? Most true, I have lost my
teeth in your service. God be with my old master; he
would not have spoke such a word.

Exeunt Orlando, Adam.

OLIVER Is it even so? Begin you to grow upon me? I will 79
physic your rankness and yet give no thousand crowns 80
neither. Holla, Dennis!

---

52 *villain* serf (Orlando quibbles on the two meanings of 'villain') **57**
railed on reviled **64** *qualities* accomplishments **67** *allottery* portion
79 *grow upon me* i.e. encroach on my place **80** *physic* cure; *rankness*
exuberant growth (cf. l. 79)

Enter Dennis.

DENNIS Calls your worship?

OLIVER Was not Charles the Duke's wrestler here to speak with me?

DENNIS So please you, he is here at the door and importunes access to you.

OLIVER Call him in. *[Exit Dennis.]* 'Twill be a good way; and to-morrow the wrestling is.

Enter Charles.

CHARLES Good morrow to your worship.

90 OLIVER Good Monsieur Charles, what's the new news at the new court?

CHARLES There's no news at the court, sir, but the old news: that is, the old Duke is banished by his younger brother the new Duke, and three or four loving lords have put themselves into voluntary exile with him, whose lands and revenues enrich the new Duke; therefore he gives them good leave to wander.

OLIVER Can you tell if Rosalind, the Duke's daughter, be banished with her father?

100 CHARLES O, no; for the Duke's daughter her cousin so loves her, being ever from their cradles bred together, that she would have followed her exile, or have died to stay behind her. She is at the court, and no less beloved of her uncle than his own daughter, and never two ladies loved as they do.

OLIVER Where will the old Duke live?

CHARLES They say he is already in the Forest of Arden, and a many merry men with him; and there they live like the old Robin Hood of England. They say many
110 young gentlemen flock to him every day, and fleet the
111 time carelessly as they did in the golden world.

OLIVER What, you wrestle to-morrow before the new Duke?

---

110 *fleet* pass   111 *the golden world* (described by Ovid in *Metamorphoses*, Book I; here men were innocent and food was plentiful)

CHARLES Marry do I, sir; and I came to acquaint you with
a matter. I am given, sir, secretly to understand that your
younger brother, Orlando, hath a disposition to come
in disguised against me to try a fall. To-morrow, sir, I 117
wrestle for my credit, and he that escapes me without 118
some broken limb shall acquit him well. Your brother is
but young and tender, and for your love I would be
loath to foil him, as I must for my own honor if he come 121
in: therefore, out of my love to you, I came hither to
acquaint you withal, that either you might stay him from
his intendment, or brook such disgrace well as he shall
run into, in that it is a thing of his own search and alto- 125
gether against my will.

OLIVER Charles, I thank thee for thy love to me, which
thou shalt find I will most kindly requite. I had myself
notice of my brother's purpose herein and have by under- 129
hand means labored to dissuade him from it; but he is
resolute. I'll tell thee, Charles, it is the stubbornest young
fellow of France; full of ambition, an envious emulator
of every man's good parts, a secret and villainous con-
triver against me his natural brother: therefore use thy
discretion. I had as lief thou didst break his neck as his
finger. And thou wert best look to't; for if thou dost
him any slight disgrace, or if he do not mightily grace 137
himself on thee, he will practise against thee by poison, 138
entrap thee by some treacherous device, and never leave
thee till he hath ta'en thy life by some indirect means or
other; for I assure thee, and almost with tears I speak it,
there is not one so young and so villainous this day living.
I speak but brotherly of him, but should I anatomize 143
him to thee as he is, I must blush and weep, and thou
must look pale and wonder.

CHARLES I am heartily glad I came hither to you. If he

---

117 *fall* bout   118 *credit* reputation   121 *foil* throw   125 *search* seeking
129 *underhand* indirect   137–38 *grace himself on thee* gain credit at your
expense   138 *practise* plot   143 *anatomize* dissect, describe

147 come to-morrow, I'll give him his payment. If ever he go
     alone again, I'll never wrestle for prize more. And so
     God keep your worship.

OLIVER Farewell, good Charles. *Exit [Charles].* Now will
     I stir this gamester. I hope I shall see an end of him ; for
     my soul, yet I know not why, hates nothing more than
153 he. Yet he's gentle, never schooled and yet learned, full
154 of noble device, of all sorts enchantingly beloved ; and
     indeed so much in the heart of the world, and especially
     of my own people, who best know him, that I am alto-
157 gether misprised. But it shall not be so long : this wrestler
     shall clear all. Nothing remains but that I kindle the boy
     thither, which now I'll go about.   *Exit.*

❉

I, ii   *Enter Rosalind and Celia.*
  1 CELIA I pray thee, Rosalind, sweet my coz, be merry.
     ROSALIND Dear Celia, I show more mirth that I am mis-
     tress of, and would you yet I were merrier ? Unless you
     could teach me to forget a banished father, you must not
  4 learn me how to remember any extraordinary pleasure.
     CELIA Herein I see thou lov'st me not with the full weight
     that I love thee. If my uncle, thy banished father, had
     banished thy uncle, the Duke my father, so thou hadst
     been still with me, I could have taught my love to take
     thy father for mine. So wouldst thou, if the truth of thy
 11 love to me were so righteously tempered as mine is to
     thee.
     ROSALIND Well, I will forget the condition of my estate
     to rejoice in yours.

147–48 *go alone* walk without help   153 *gentle* possessed of the qualities of a
gentleman   154 *device* designs; *enchantingly* as by enchantment   157
misprised scorned
I, ii The grounds of Duke Frederick's palace   1 *coz* cousin   4 *learn* teach
11 *righteously tempered* properly composed

CELIA You know my father hath no child but I, nor none
is like to have; and truly, when he dies, thou shalt be his
heir; for what he hath taken away from thy father per- 17
force, I will render thee again in affection. By mine
honor, I will, and when I break that oath, let me turn
monster. Therefore, my sweet Rose, my dear Rose, be
merry.

ROSALIND From henceforth I will, coz, and devise sports.
Let me see, what think you of falling in love?

CELIA Marry, I prithee do, to make sport withal; but love
no man in good earnest, nor no further in sport neither
than with safety of a pure blush thou mayst in honor 26
come off again. 27

ROSALIND What shall be our sport then?

CELIA Let us sit and mock the good housewife Fortune 29
from her wheel, that her gifts may henceforth be be- 30
stowed equally.

ROSALIND I would we could do so, for her benefits are
mightily misplaced, and the bountiful blind woman
doth most mistake in her gifts to women.

CELIA 'Tis true, for those that she makes fair she scarce
makes honest, and those that she makes honest she 36
makes very ill-favoredly.

ROSALIND Nay, now thou goest from Fortune's office to
Nature's. Fortune reigns in gifts of the world, not in the
lineaments of Nature. 40

        Enter [Touchstone, the] Clown.

CELIA No; when Nature hath made a fair creature, may
she not by Fortune fall into the fire? Though Nature
hath given us wit to flout at Fortune, hath not Fortune
sent in this fool to cut off the argument?

---

17 *perforce* forcibly 26 *pure* innocent 27 *come off* get away 29 *good
housewife* i.e. one who spins 30 *her wheel* (which carried some up, others
down) 36 *honest* chaste 40 s.d. *Touchstone* (his name means a kind of
flint used to test for gold and silver by the color of the streak made when
rubbed across metal)

ROSALIND Indeed, there is Fortune too hard for Nature
46   when Fortune makes Nature's natural the cutter-off of
Nature's wit.

CELIA Peradventure this is not Fortune's work neither,
but Nature's, who perceiveth our natural wits too dull to
reason of such goddesses and hath sent this natural for
our whetstone, for always the dullness of the fool is the
whetstone of the wits. How now, wit; whither wander
you?

TOUCHSTONE Mistress, you must come away to your
father.

CELIA Were you made the messenger?

TOUCHSTONE No, by mine honor, but I was bid to come
for you.

ROSALIND Where learned you that oath, fool?

TOUCHSTONE Of a certain knight that swore by his honor
they were good pancakes, and swore by his honor the
mustard was naught. Now I'll stand to it, the pancakes
were naught, and the mustard was good, and yet was
63   not the knight forsworn.

CELIA How prove you that in the great heap of your
knowledge?

ROSALIND Ay, marry, now unmuzzle your wisdom.

TOUCHSTONE Stand you both forth now. Stroke your
chins, and swear by your beards that I am a knave.

CELIA By our beards, if we had them, thou art.

TOUCHSTONE By my knavery, if I had it, then I were;
but if you swear by that that is not, you are not forsworn; no more was this knight, swearing by his honor,
for he never had any; or if he had, he had sworn it away
before ever he saw those pancakes or that mustard.

CELIA Prithee, who is't that thou mean'st?

TOUCHSTONE One that old Frederick, your father, loves.

CELIA My father's love is enough to honor him enough:

46 *natural* born fool   63 *forsworn* falsely sworn

speak no more of him; you'll be whipped for taxation 78
one of these days.

TOUCHSTONE The more pity that fools may not speak
wisely what wise men do foolishly.

CELIA By my troth, thou sayest true, for since the little
wit that fools have was silenced, the little foolery that
wise men have makes a great show. Here comes Monsieur Le Beau.

    Enter Le Beau.

ROSALIND With his mouth full of news.

CELIA Which he will put on us as pigeons feed their 87
young.

ROSALIND Then shall we be news-crammed.

CELIA All the better; we shall be the more marketable.
Bon jour, Monsieur Le Beau, what's the news?

LE BEAU Fair princess, you have lost much good sport.

CELIA Sport; of what color?   92

LE BEAU What color, madam? How shall I answer you?

ROSALIND As wit and fortune will.

TOUCHSTONE Or as the destinies decree.

CELIA Well said; that was laid on with a trowel.   96

TOUCHSTONE Nay, if I keep not my rank –   97

ROSALIND Thou losest thy old smell.

LE BEAU You amaze me, ladies. I would have told you of 99
good wrestling, which you have lost the sight of.

ROSALIND Yet tell us the manner of the wrestling.

LE BEAU I will tell you the beginning; and if it please your
ladyships, you may see the end, for the best is yet to do,
and here, where you are, they are coming to perform it.

CELIA Well, the beginning that is dead and buried.

LE BEAU There comes an old man and his three sons.

CELIA I could match this beginning with an old tale.

LE BEAU Three proper young men, of excellent growth
and presence.

---

78 *taxation* slander **87** *put on* force upon **92** *color* sort **96** *with a trowel*
i.e. slapped on thickly **97** *my rank* i.e. my rating as a witty person **99**
amaze confuse

110 ROSALIND With bills on their necks, 'Be it known unto all men by these presents.'

LE BEAU The eldest of the three wrestled with Charles, the Duke's wrestler; which Charles in a moment threw him and broke three of his ribs, that there is little hope of life in him. So he served the second, and so the third. Yonder they lie, the poor old man, their father, making

117 such pitiful dole over them that all the beholders take his part with weeping.

ROSALIND Alas!

TOUCHSTONE But what is the sport, monsieur, that the ladies have lost?

LE BEAU Why, this that I speak of.

TOUCHSTONE Thus men may grow wiser every day. It is the first time that ever I heard breaking of ribs was sport for ladies.

CELIA Or I, I promise thee.

127 ROSALIND But is there any else longs to see this broken music in his sides? Is there yet another dotes upon rib-breaking? Shall we see this wrestling, cousin?

LE BEAU You must, if you stay here, for here is the place appointed for the wrestling, and they are ready to perform it.

CELIA Yonder sure they are coming. Let us now stay and see it.

> *Flourish. Enter Duke [Frederick], Lords, Orlando, Charles, and Attendants.*

DUKE FREDERICK Come on. Since the youth will not be

136 entreated, his own peril on his forwardness.

ROSALIND Is yonder the man?

LE BEAU Even he, madam.

139 CELIA Alas, he is too young; yet he looks successfully.

DUKE FREDERICK How now, daughter and cousin; are you crept hither to see the wrestling?

110 *bills* notices   117 *dole* lament   127–28 *broken music* wrong arrangement of parts   136 *forwardness* rashness   139 *successfully* likely to succeed

ROSALIND Ay, my liege, so please you give us leave.

DUKE FREDERICK You will take little delight in it, I can
tell you, there is such odds in the man. In pity of the 144
challenger's youth I would fain dissuade him, but he
will not be entreated. Speak to him, ladies; see if you
can move him.

CELIA Call him hither, good Monsieur Le Beau.

DUKE FREDERICK Do so. I'll not be by.
    [Steps aside.]

LE BEAU Monsieur the challenger, the princess calls for 150
you.

ORLANDO I attend them with all respect and duty.

ROSALIND Young man, have you challenged Charles the
wrestler?

ORLANDO No, fair princess. He is the general challenger;
I come but in as others do, to try with him the strength
of my youth.

CELIA Young gentleman, your spirits are too bold for
your years. You have seen cruel proof of this man's
strength; if you saw yourself with your eyes or knew
yourself with your judgment, the fear of your adventure
would counsel you to a more equal enterprise. We pray
you for your own sake to embrace your own safety and
give over this attempt.

ROSALIND Do, young sir. Your reputation shall not
therefore be misprised; we will make it our suit to the 165
Duke that the wrestling might not go forward.

ORLANDO I beseech you, punish me not with your hard
thoughts, wherein I confess me much guilty to deny so
fair and excellent ladies anything. But let your fair eyes
and gentle wishes go with me to my trial; wherein if I be
foiled, there is but one shamed that was never gracious; 171
if killed, but one dead that is willing to be so. I shall do
my friends no wrong, for I have none to lament me; the
world no injury, for in it I have nothing. Only in the

144 *odds* superiority 150 *princess* (taken as plural by Orlando) 165 *misprised* undervalued 171 *gracious* graced by fortune

world I fill up a place, which may be better supplied
when I have made it empty.

ROSALIND The little strength that I have, I would it were
with you.

CELIA And mine to eke out hers.

180 ROSALIND Fare you well. Pray heaven I be deceived in
you!

CELIA Your heart's desires be with you!

CHARLES Come, where is this young gallant that is so
desirous to lie with his mother earth?

ORLANDO Ready, sir; but his will hath in it a more
185 modest working.

DUKE FREDERICK You shall try but one fall.

CHARLES No, I warrant your Grace you shall not entreat
him to a second that have so mightily persuaded him
from a first.

ORLANDO You mean to mock me after. You should not
191 have mocked me before. But come your ways.

192 ROSALIND Now Hercules be thy speed, young man!

CELIA I would I were invisible, to catch the strong fellow
by the leg.

> *Wrestle.*

ROSALIND O excellent young man!

196 CELIA If I had a thunderbolt in mine eye, I can tell who
should down.

> *[Charles is thrown.] Shout.*

DUKE FREDERICK No more, no more.

199 ORLANDO Yes, I beseech your Grace; I am not yet well
breathed.

DUKE FREDERICK
How dost thou, Charles?

LE BEAU   He cannot speak, my lord.

180–81 *deceived in you* mistaken in my view of your abilities **185** *working*
undertaking **191** *come your ways* come on **192** *Hercules* (symbol of
strength); *be thy speed* favor you **196** *If . . . eye* if I could cast a thunderbolt
with my eyes **199–200** *well breathed* warmed up

DUKE FREDERICK

Bear him away.

[Charles is borne out.]

What is thy name, young man ?

ORLANDO Orlando, my liege, the youngest son of Sir
Rowland de Boys.

DUKE FREDERICK

I would thou hadst been son to some man else.

The world esteemed thy father honorable,

But I did find him still mine enemy.   207

Thou shouldst have better pleased me with this deed

Hadst thou descended from another house.

But fare thee well ; thou art a gallant youth ;

I would thou hadst told me of another father.

Exit Duke [, with Train].

CELIA

Were I my father, coz, would I do this ?

ORLANDO

I am more proud to be Sir Rowland's son,

His youngest son, and would not change that calling   214

To be adopted heir to Frederick.

ROSALIND

My father loved Sir Rowland as his soul,

And all the world was of my father's mind.

Had I before known this young man his son,

I should have given him tears unto entreaties

Ere he should thus have ventured.

CELIA   Gentle cousin,

Let us go thank him and encourage him.

My father's rough and envious disposition

Sticks me at heart. Sir, you have well deserved ;   223

If you do keep your promises in love

But justly as you have exceeded all promise,

Your mistress shall be happy.

207 *still* constantly   **214** *calling* title   **223** *Sticks* stabs

226 ROSALIND   Gentleman,
          [Gives chain.]
227   Wear this for me, one out of suits with fortune,
          That could give more but that her hand lacks means.
          Shall we go, coz?
     CELIA   Ay. Fare you well, fair gentleman.
     ORLANDO
230   Can I not say 'I thank you'? My better parts
          Are all thrown down, and that which here stands up
232   Is but a quintain, a mere lifeless block.
     ROSALIND
          He calls us back. My pride fell with my fortunes;
          I'll ask him what he would. Did you call, sir?
          Sir, you have wrestled well, and overthrown
          More than your enemies.
     CELIA   Will you go, coz?
     ROSALIND
237   Have with you. Fare you well.   *Exit [with Celia].*
     ORLANDO
          What passion hangs these weights upon my tongue?
239   I cannot speak to her, yet she urged conference.
               Enter Le Beau.
          O poor Orlando, thou art overthrown!
          Or Charles or something weaker masters thee.
     LE BEAU
          Good sir, I do in friendship counsel you
          To leave this place. Albeit you have deserved
          High commendation, true applause, and love,
245   Yet such is now the Duke's condition
246   That he misconsters all that you have done.
247   The Duke is humorous. What he is, indeed,
          More suits you to conceive than I to speak of.

---

226 s.d. *chain* (see III, ii, 172)   227 *suits* favor   230 *better parts* i.e. composure and manners   232 *quintain* post with crossbars for tilting   237 *Have with you* come on   239 *urged conference* invited conversation   245 *condition* disposition   246 *misconsters* misconstrues   247 *humorous* subject to emotional disturbances

ORLANDO
I thank you, sir ; and pray you tell me this :
Which of the two was daughter of the Duke,
That here was at the wrestling ?

LE BEAU
Neither his daughter, if we judge by manners,
But yet indeed the taller is his daughter,   253
The other is daughter to the banished Duke,
And here detained by her usurping uncle
To keep his daughter company, whose loves
Are dearer than the natural bond of sisters.
But I can tell you that of late this Duke
Hath ta'en displeasure 'gainst his gentle niece,
Grounded upon no other argument   260
But that the people praise her for her virtues
And pity her for her good father's sake ;
And, on my life, his malice 'gainst the lady
Will suddenly break forth. Sir, fare you well.
Hereafter, in a better world than this,   265
I shall desire more love and knowledge of you.

ORLANDO
I rest much bounden to you. Fare you well.
                              [Exit Le Beau.]
Thus must I from the smoke into the smother,   268
From tyrant Duke unto a tyrant brother.
But heavenly Rosalind !   *Exit.*

*

Enter Celia and Rosalind.   I, iii

CELIA Why, cousin, why, Rosalind ! Cupid have mercy,
not a word ?
ROSALIND Not one to throw at a dog.

---

253 *taller* (either Le Beau or Shakespeare is here confused ; Rosalind, not
Celia, is later shown to be the taller) 260 *argument* reason 265 *world*
state of affairs 268 *smother* suffocation
I, iii Duke Frederick's palace

CELIA No, thy words are too precious to be cast away
5   upon curs; throw some of them at me; come, lame me
with reasons.

ROSALIND Then there were two cousins laid up, when
the one should be lamed with reasons and the other mad
without any.

CELIA But is all this for your father?

ROSALIND No, some of it is for my child's father. O, how
full of briers is this working-day world!

CELIA They are but burrs, cousin, thrown upon thee in
holiday foolery; if we walk not in the trodden paths,
our very petticoats will catch them.

ROSALIND I could shake them off my coat; these burrs
are in my heart.

18 CELIA Hem them away.

19 ROSALIND I would try, if I could cry 'hem,' and have
him.

CELIA Come, come, wrestle with thy affections.

ROSALIND O, they take the part of a better wrestler than
myself!

23 CELIA O, a good wish upon you! You will try in time, in
24   despite of a fall. But turning these jests out of service,
let us talk in good earnest. Is it possible on such a sudden you should fall into so strong a liking with old Sir
Rowland's youngest son?

ROSALIND The Duke my father loved his father dearly.

CELIA Doth it therefore ensue that you should love his son
30   dearly? By this kind of chase, I should hate him, for my
father hated his father dearly; yet I hate not Orlando.

ROSALIND No, faith, hate him not, for my sake.

33 CELIA Why should I not? Doth he not deserve well?
          Enter Duke [Frederick], with Lords.

5–6 *lame me with reasons* injure me with explanations   **18** *Hem* tuck   **19**
cry 'hem' clear the throat   **23** *try* make trial (as *wrestler?*)   **24** *fall* (a
quibble on this word)   **30** *chase* argument   **33** *deserve well* i.e. to be hated
(but Rosalind ignores the implied conclusion)

ROSALIND Let me love him for that, and do you love him
    because I do. Look, here comes the Duke.
CELIA With his eyes full of anger.
DUKE FREDERICK
    Mistress, dispatch you with your safest haste   37
    And get you from our court.
ROSALIND   Me, uncle?
DUKE FREDERICK   You, cousin.
    Within these ten days if that thou beest found
    So near our public court as twenty miles,
    Thou diest for it.
ROSALIND   I do beseech your Grace
    Let me the knowledge of my fault bear with me.
    If with myself I hold intelligence   43
    Or have acquaintance with mine own desires,
    If that I do not dream or be not frantic,   45
    As I do trust I am not; then, dear uncle,
    Never so much as in a thought unborn
    Did I offend your Highness.
DUKE FREDERICK   Thus do all traitors.
    If their purgation did consist in words,   49
    They are as innocent as grace itself.   50
    Let it suffice thee that I trust thee not.
ROSALIND
    Yet your mistrust cannot make me a traitor.
    Tell me whereon the likelihoods depends.   53
DUKE FREDERICK
    Thou art thy father's daughter, there's enough.
ROSALIND
    So was I when your Highness took his dukedom;
    So was I when your Highness banished him.
    Treason is not inherited, my lord,
    Or if we did derive it from our friends,   58

---

37 *safest haste* i.e. the hastier the safer 43 *hold intelligence* am in com-
munication 45 *frantic* insane 49 *purgation* exoneration 50 *grace* virtue
53 *likelihoods* i.e. suspicion 58 *friends* kin

What's that to me? My father was no traitor.
Then, good my liege, mistake me not so much
To think my poverty is treacherous.

CELIA
Dear sovereign, hear me speak.

DUKE FREDERICK
Ay, Celia. We stayed her for your sake,
Else had she with her father ranged along.

CELIA
I did not then entreat to have her stay;
66   It was your pleasure and your own remorse.
I was too young that time to value her,
But now I know her. If she be a traitor,
Why, so am I. We still have slept together,
Rose at an instant, learned, played, eat together;
71   And wheresoe'er we went, like Juno's swans,
Still we went coupled and inseparable.

DUKE FREDERICK
73   She is too subtile for thee; and her smoothness,
Her very silence and her patience,
Speak to the people, and they pity her.
Thou art a fool. She robs thee of thy name,
77   And thou wilt show more bright and seem more virtuous
When she is gone. Then open not thy lips.
Firm and irrevocable is my doom
Which I have passed upon her; she is banished.

CELIA
Pronounce that sentence then on me, my liege;
I cannot live out of her company.

DUKE FREDERICK
You are a fool. You, niece, provide yourself;
If you outstay the time, upon mine honor,
85   And in the greatness of my word, you die.

                                        Exit Duke, &c.

66 *remorse* compunction   71 *Juno's swans* (according to Ovid it was Venus
who was drawn through the air by a pair of swans)   73 *subtile* crafty   77
virtuous possessed of good qualities   85 *greatness* authority

CELIA
O my poor Rosalind, whither wilt thou go?
Wilt thou change fathers? I will give thee mine.
I charge thee be not thou more grieved than I am.

ROSALIND
I have more cause.

CELIA   Thou hast not, cousin.
Prithee be cheerful. Know'st thou not the Duke
Hath banished me, his daughter?

ROSALIND   That he hath not.

CELIA
No? hath not? Rosalind lacks then the love
Which teacheth thee that thou and I am one.
Shall we be sund'red, shall we part, sweet girl?
No, let my father seek another heir.
Therefore devise with me how we may fly,   96
Whither to go, and what to bear with us;
And do not seek to take your change upon you,   98
To bear your griefs yourself and leave me out;
For, by this heaven, now at our sorrows pale,
Say what thou canst, I'll go along with thee.

ROSALIND
Why, whither shall we go?

CELIA
To seek my uncle in the Forest of Arden.

ROSALIND
Alas, what danger will it be to us,
Maids as we are, to travel forth so far!
Beauty provoketh thieves sooner than gold.

CELIA
I'll put myself in poor and mean attire
And with a kind of umber smirch my face;   108
The like do you; so shall we pass along
And never stir assailants.

ROSALIND   Were it not better,

96 *devise* plan   98 *change* i.e. of fortunes   108 *umber* brown earth

45

Because that I am more than common tall,
112 That I did suit me all points like a man?
113 A gallant curtle-axe upon my thigh,
A boar-spear in my hand; and, in my heart
Lie there what hidden woman's fear there will,
116 We'll have a swashing and a martial outside,
117 As many other mannish cowards have
118 That do outface it with their semblances.

CELIA
What shall I call thee when thou art a man?

ROSALIND
I'll have no worse a name than Jove's own page,
121 And therefore look you call me Ganymede.
But what will you be called?

CELIA
Something that hath a reference to my state:
124 No longer Celia, but Aliena.

ROSALIND
125 But, cousin, what if we assayed to steal
The clownish fool out of your father's court;
Would he not be a comfort to our travel?

CELIA
He'll go along o'er the wide world with me;
129 Leave me alone to woo him. Let's away
And get our jewels and our wealth together,
Devise the fittest time and safest way
To hide us from pursuit that will be made
After my flight. Now go in we content
To liberty, and not to banishment.   *Exeunt.*

*

112 *suit me all points* dress completely   113 *curtle-axe* curved sword   116
swashing blustering   117 *mannish* i.e. pretending manliness   118 *outface it*
bluff   121 *Ganymede* (who for his beauty was made cupbearer to Jove)
124 *Aliena* i.e. estranged   125 *assayed* undertook   129 *woo* coax

Enter Duke Senior, Amiens, and two or three Lords, **II, i**
like Foresters.

DUKE SENIOR

Now, my co-mates and brothers in exile,
Hath not old custom made this life more sweet
Than that of painted pomp? Are not these woods
More free from peril than the envious court?
Here feel we not the penalty of Adam;   5
The seasons' difference, as the icy fang   6
And churlish chiding of the winter's wind,   7
Which, when it bites and blows upon my body
Even till I shrink with cold, I smile and say
'This is no flattery'; these are counsellors
That feelingly persuade me what I am.
Sweet are the uses of adversity,
Which, like the toad, ugly and venomous,   13
Wears yet a precious jewel in his head;
And this our life, exempt from public haunt,   15
Finds tongues in trees, books in the running brooks,
Sermons in stones, and good in everything.

AMIENS

I would not change it; happy is your Grace
That can translate the stubbornness of fortune   19
Into so quiet and so sweet a style.

DUKE SENIOR

Come, shall we go and kill us venison?
And yet it irks me the poor dappled fools,   22
Being native burghers of this desert city,   23
Should, in their own confines, with forkèd heads   24
Have their round haunches gored.

1. LORD   Indeed, my lord,

II, i The Forest of Arden   **5** *not* (frequently emended to 'but'); *penalty of Adam* loss of innocence, expulsion from Garden of Eden (see Genesis iii) **6** *as* for example   **7** *churlish* rough   **13-14** *toad . . . head* ('The foul toad hath a fair stone in his head.' Lyly, *Euphues*)   **15** *haunt* society   **19** *stubbornness* hardness   **22** *fools* pitiable creatures   **23** *desert* uninhabited (rather than devoid of vegetation)   **24** *confines* territory; *forkèd heads* barbed arrowheads

The melancholy Jaques grieves at that,
27 And in that kind swears you do more usurp
Than doth your brother that hath banished you.
To-day my Lord of Amiens and myself
Did steal behind him as he lay along
Under an oak, whose antique root peeps out
32 Upon the brook that brawls along this wood,
33 To the which place a poor sequest'red stag
That from the hunter's aim had ta'en a hurt
Did come to languish ; and indeed, my lord,
The wretched animal heaved forth such groans
That their discharge did stretch his leathern coat
38 Almost to bursting, and the big round tears
Coursed one another down his innocent nose
In piteous chase ; and thus the hairy fool,
Much markèd of the melancholy Jaques,
Stood on th' extremest verge of the swift brook,
Augmenting it with tears.

DUKE SENIOR   But what said Jaques ?
44 Did he not moralize this spectacle ?

1. LORD
O, yes, into a thousand similes.
46 First, for his weeping into the needless stream :
'Poor deer,' quoth he, 'thou mak'st a testament
As worldlings do, giving thy sum of more
To that which had too much.' Then, being there alone,
50 Left and abandoned of his velvet friend :
''Tis right,' quoth he, 'thus misery doth part
52 The flux of company.' Anon a careless herd,
Full of the pasture, jumps along by him
And never stays to greet him ; 'Ay,' quoth Jaques,
'Sweep on, you fat and greasy citizens,
'Tis just the fashion ; wherefore do you look

---

27 *kind* way   32 *brawls* makes noisy sounds   33 *sequest'red* separated
38 *tears* (wounded deer were commonly supposed to shed tears)   44
moralize draw a moral from   46 *needless* needing no more water   50 *velvet*
in the 'velvet' stage   52 *flux* confluence

Upon that poor and broken bankrupt there?'
Thus most invectively he pierceth through
The body of the country, city, court,
Yea, and of this our life, swearing that we
Are mere usurpers, tyrants, and what's worse,
To fright the animals and to kill them up   62
In their assigned and native dwelling place.   63

DUKE SENIOR
And did you leave him in this contemplation?

2. LORD
We did, my lord, weeping and commenting
Upon the sobbing deer.

DUKE SENIOR   Show me the place.
I love to cope him in these sullen fits,   67
For then he's full of matter.

1. LORD
I'll bring you to him straight.   *Exeunt.*

*

Enter Duke [Frederick], with Lords.   II, ii

DUKE FREDERICK
Can it be possible that no man saw them?
It cannot be; some villains of my court
Are of consent and sufferance in this.   3

1. LORD
I cannot hear of any that did see her.
The ladies her attendants of her chamber
Saw her abed, and in the morning early
They found the bed untreasured of their mistress.

2. LORD
My lord, the roynish clown at whom so oft   8
Your Grace was wont to laugh is also missing.
Hisperia, the princess' gentlewoman,

62 *up* off   63 *assigned* i.e. in the natural order   67 *cope* cope with
II, ii Duke Frederick's palace   3 *of consent and sufferance* in connivance
8 *roynish* scurvy

49

Confesses that she secretly o'erheard
Your daughter and her cousin much commend
13   The parts and graces of the wrestler
That did but lately foil the sinewy Charles,
And she believes, wherever they are gone,
That youth is surely in their company.

DUKE FREDERICK
Send to his brother, fetch that gallant hither;
If he be absent, bring his brother to me;
19   I'll make him find him. Do this suddenly,
20   And let not search and inquisition quail
To bring again these foolish runaways.   *Exeunt.*

*

II, iii   *Enter Orlando and Adam.*

ORLANDO
Who's there?

ADAM
What, my young master, O my gentle master,
3   O my sweet master, O you memory
Of old Sir Rowland, why, what make you here?
Why are you virtuous? Why do people love you?
And wherefore are you gentle, strong, and valiant?
7   Why would you be so fond to overcome
8   The bonny prizer of the humorous Duke?
Your praise is come too swiftly home before you.
Know you not, master, to some kind of men
Their graces serve them but as enemies?
12   No more do yours. Your virtues, gentle master,
Are sanctified and holy traitors to you.

---

13 *parts* good qualities   **19** *suddenly* at once   **20** *inquisition quail* enquiry falter
II, iii Before Oliver's house   **3** *memory* living memorial   **7** *fond* foolish
8 *bonny prizer* sturdy prize-fighter; *humorous* temperamental, capricious
12 *No more* no better   **12–13** *Your virtues . . . to you* i.e. Orlando's virtues, although worthy of religious approval, have only worked against him in the mind of his brother

O, what a world is this, when what is comely
Envenoms him that bears it !

ORLANDO
Why, what's the matter ?

ADAM   O unhappy youth,
Come not within these doors ; within this roof
The enemy of all your graces lives.
Your brother, no, no brother, yet the son
(Yet not the son, I will not call him son)
Of him I was about to call his father,
Hath heard your praises, and this night he means
To burn the lodging where you use to lie   23
And you within it. If he fail of that,
He will have other means to cut you off.
I overheard him, and his practices ;   26
This is no place, this house is but a butchery ;
Abhor it, fear it, do not enter it !

ORLANDO
Why, whither, Adam, wouldst thou have me go ?

ADAM
No matter whither, so you come not here.

ORLANDO
What, wouldst thou have me go and beg my food,
Or with a base and boist'rous sword enforce
A thievish living on the common road ?
This I must do, or know not what to do ;
Yet this I will not do, do how I can.
I rather will subject me to the malice
Of a diverted blood and bloody brother.   37

ADAM
But do not so. I have five hundred crowns,
The thrifty hire I saved under your father,   39
Which I did store to be my foster nurse
When service should in my old limbs lie lame   41

---

23 *use* are accustomed   **26** *practices* plots   **37** *diverted* i.e. from natural
affection   **39** *thrifty hire I saved* wages I thriftily saved   **41** *service . . . lame*
ability to serve should be weakened by old age

And unregarded age in corners thrown.
43   Take that, and he that doth the ravens feed,
Yea, providently caters for the sparrow,
Be comfort to my age. Here is the gold,
All this I give you. Let me be your servant;
Though I look old, yet I am strong and lusty,
For in my youth I never did apply
49   Hot and rebellious liquors in my blood,
50   Nor did not with unbashful forehead woo
The means of weakness and debility;
Therefore my age is as a lusty winter,
Frosty, but kindly. Let me go with you;
I'll do the service of a younger man
In all your business and necessities.

ORLANDO

O good old man, how well in thee appears
57   The constant service of the antique world,
58   When service sweat for duty, not for meed!
Thou art not for the fashion of these times,
Where none will sweat but for promotion,
61   And having that, do choke their service up
Even with the having; it is not so with thee.
But, poor old man, thou prun'st a rotten tree
That cannot so much as a blossom yield
65   In lieu of all thy pains and husbandry.
But come thy ways, we'll go along together,
And ere we have thy youthful wages spent,
68   We'll light upon some settled low content.

ADAM

Master, go on, and I will follow thee
To the last gasp with truth and loyalty.

43–44 *ravens . . . sparrow* (see Psalms cxlvii, 9; Luke xii, 6)   49 *rebellious* causing rebellion against self-control   50 *unbashful forehead* shameless face   57 *constant* faithful   58 *meed* reward   61–62 *do choke . . . having* cease their service on gaining promotion   65 *In lieu of* in return for   68 *low content* humble contentment

From seventeen years till now almost fourscore
Here livèd I, but now live here no more;
At seventeen years many their fortunes seek,
But at fourscore it is too late a week;   74
Yet fortune cannot recompense me better
Than to die well and not my master's debtor.   *Exeunt.*

*

Enter Rosalind for Ganymede, Celia for Aliena,   II, iv
and Clown, alias Touchstone.

ROSALIND O Jupiter, how merry are my spirits!   1

TOUCHSTONE I care not for my spirits if my legs were
not weary.

ROSALIND I could find in my heart to disgrace my man's
apparel and to cry like a woman; but I must comfort the
weaker vessel, as doublet and hose ought to show itself 6
courageous to petticoat. Therefore, courage, good
Aliena!

CELIA I pray you bear with me; I cannot go no further.

TOUCHSTONE For my part, I had rather bear with you
than bear you; yet I should bear no cross if I did bear 11
you; for I think you have no money in your purse.

ROSALIND Well, this is the Forest of Arden.

TOUCHSTONE Ay, now am I in Arden, the more fool I.
When I was at home, I was in a better place, but travel-
lers must be content.
Enter Corin and Silvius.

ROSALIND
Ay, be so, good Touchstone. Look you, who comes here,
A young man and an old in solemn talk.

CORIN
That is the way to make her scorn you still.

---

74 *week* time
II, iv The Forest of Arden 1 *merry* (presumably ironic; often emended
to 'weary') 6 *doublet and hose* jacket and breeches 11 *cross* (1) burden,
(2) penny, which had a cross stamped on it (a stock pun)

SILVIUS

O Corin, that thou knew'st how I do love her!

CORIN

I partly guess, for I have loved ere now.

SILVIUS

No, Corin, being old, thou canst not guess,
Though in thy youth thou wast as true a lover
As ever sighed upon a midnight pillow.
But if thy love were ever like to mine,
As sure I think did never man love so,
How many actions most ridiculous
28   Hast thou been drawn to by thy fantasy?

CORIN

Into a thousand that I have forgotten.

SILVIUS

O, thou didst then never love so heartily!
If thou rememb'rest not the slightest folly
That ever love did make thee run into,
Thou hast not loved.
Or if thou hast not sat as I do now,
35   Wearing thy hearer in thy mistress' praise,
Thou hast not loved.
Or if thou hast not broke from company
Abruptly, as my passion now makes me,
Thou hast not loved. O Phebe, Phebe, Phebe!   *Exit*.

ROSALIND

40   Alas, poor shepherd! Searching of thy wound,
I have by hard adventure found mine own.

TOUCHSTONE And I mine. I remember, when I was in
love I broke my sword upon a stone and bid him take
that for coming a-night to Jane Smile; and I remember
45   the kissing of her batler, and the cow's dugs that her
46   pretty chopt hands had milked; and I remember the
47   wooing of a peascod instead of her, from whom I took

28 *fantasy* (Corin's love is likened to a mere fancy)   35 *Wearing* wearying
40 *Searching* probing   45 *batler* bat used in washing clothes   46 *chopt*
chapped   47 *peascod* pea pod (here used for whole plant)

two cods, and giving her them again, said with weeping
tears, 'Wear these for my sake.' We that are true lovers
run into strange capers; but as all is mortal in nature, so
is all nature in love mortal in folly.   51

ROSALIND Thou speak'st wiser than thou art ware of.   52

TOUCHSTONE Nay, I shall ne'er be ware of mine own
wit till I break my shins against it.

ROSALIND
Jove, Jove! this shepherd's passion
Is much upon my fashion.

TOUCHSTONE
And mine, but it grows something stale with me.

CELIA
I pray you, one of you question yond man
If he for gold will give us any food.
I faint almost to death.

TOUCHSTONE   Holla, you clown!   61

ROSALIND
Peace, fool! he's not thy kinsman.

CORIN
Who calls?

TOUCHSTONE Your betters, sir.

CORIN   Else are they very wretched.

ROSALIND
Peace, I say! Good even to you, friend.

CORIN
And to you, gentle sir, and to you all.

ROSALIND
I prithee, shepherd, if that love or gold
Can in this desert place buy entertainment,   67
Bring us where we may rest ourselves and feed.
Here's a young maid with travel much oppressed,
And faints for succor.

CORIN   Fair sir, I pity her

---

51 *mortal in folly* i.e. by its foolishness shows its human nature, which is
subject to mortality 52 *ware* aware 61 *clown* yokel 67 *desert* uninhabited; *entertainment* food and lodging

And wish, for her sake more than for mine own,
My fortunes were more able to relieve her;
But I am shepherd to another man
And do not shear the fleeces that I graze.
My master is of churlish disposition
76   And little recks to find the way to heaven
By doing deeds of hospitality.
78   Besides, his cote, his flocks, and bounds of feed
Are now on sale, and at our sheepcote now,
By reason of his absence, there is nothing
That you will feed on; but what is, come see,
82   And in my voice most welcome shall you be.

ROSALIND
What is he that shall buy his flock and pasture?

CORIN
That young swain that you saw here but erewhile,
That little cares for buying anything.

ROSALIND
86   I pray thee, if it stand with honesty,
Buy thou the cottage, pasture, and the flock,
88   And thou shalt have to pay for it of us.

CELIA
89   And we will mend thy wages. I like this place
90   And willingly could waste my time in it.

CORIN
Assuredly the thing is to be sold.
92   Go with me; if you like upon report
The soil, the profit, and this kind of life,
94   I will your very faithful feeder be
And buy it with your gold right suddenly.   *Exeunt.*

❉

76 *recks* reckons   78 *cote* cottage; *bounds of feed* pastures   82 *in my voice* as
far as I have any influence   86 *if . . . honesty* if it is consistent with
honorable dealing   88 *have to pay* have the money to pay   89 *mend* im-
prove   90 *waste* spend   92 *report* further information   94 *feeder* servant

Enter Amiens, Jaques, and others.

Song.

[AMIENS]   Under the greenwood tree
              Who loves to lie with me,
            And turn his merry note   3
              Unto the sweet bird's throat,
          Come hither, come hither, come hither.
            Here shall he see no enemy
          But winter and rough weather.

JAQUES More, more, I prithee more!

AMIENS It will make you melancholy, Monsieur Jaques.

JAQUES I thank it. More, I prithee more! I can suck
melancholy out of a song as a weasel sucks eggs. More, I
prithee more!

AMIENS My voice is ragged. I know I cannot please you.

JAQUES I do not desire you to please me; I do desire you to
sing. Come, more, another stanzo! Call you 'em stan-
zos?

AMIENS What you will, Monsieur Jaques.

JAQUES Nay, I care not for their names; they owe me
nothing. Will you sing?

AMIENS More at your request than to please myself.

JAQUES Well then, if ever I thank any man, I'll thank
you. But that they call compliment is like th' encounter   21
of two dog-apes, and when a man thanks me heartily,   22
methinks I have given him a penny and he renders me
the beggarly thanks. Come, sing; and you that will not,   24
hold your tongues.

AMIENS Well, I'll end the song. Sirs, cover the while; the   26
Duke will drink under this tree. He hath been all this
day to look you.   28

II, v The Forest   3 *turn* attune   21 *compliment* politeness   21–22 *th'*
encounter . . . dog apes i.e. a mutual mockery   22 *dog-apes* baboons   24
beggarly effusive, like a beggar's   26 *cover the while* meanwhile set the cloth
for a meal   28 *to look* looking for

JAQUES And I have been all this day to avoid him. He is
too disputable for my company. I think of as many
matters as he, but I give heaven thanks and make no
boast of them. Come, warble, come.

Song.

All together here.

Who doth ambition shun
 And loves to live i' th' sun,
Seeking the food he eats,
 And pleased with what he gets,
Come hither, come hither, come hither.
 Here shall he see no enemy
 But winter and rough weather.

40 JAQUES I'll give you a verse to this note that I made
41 yesterday in despite of my invention.
AMIENS And I'll sing it.
JAQUES Thus it goes.
  [Gives paper.]
44 AMIENS If it do come to pass
    That any man turn ass,
    Leaving his wealth and ease
    A stubborn will to please,
48   Ducdame, ducdame, ducdame.
    Here shall he see gross fools as he,
    An if he will come to me.

What's that 'ducdame'?
JAQUES 'Tis a Greek invocation to call fools into a circle.
I'll go sleep, if I can; if I cannot, I'll rail against all the
54 first-born of Egypt.

---

40 *note* tune 41 *in . . . invention* although I lack imagination 44 *Amiens*
(song sung by Jaques in second folio and many modern editions) 48 *Ducdame* (trisyllabic; variously explained as deriving from gypsy 'dukrā mē,' a
fortuneteller's cry to the gullible; from Welsh 'dwech 'da mi,' meaning
'come with me'; etc.) 54 *first-born of Egypt* (whose death finally resulted
in sending the Israelites into the wilderness; see Exodus xi, xii)

AMIENS And I'll go seek the Duke. His banquet is prepared.   *Exeunt.*

*

Enter Orlando and Adam.   II, vi

ADAM Dear master, I can go no further. O, I die for food.
Here lie I down and measure out my grave. Farewell,
kind master.

ORLANDO Why, how now, Adam? no greater heart in
thee? Live a little, comfort a little, cheer thyself a little.
If this uncouth forest yield anything savage, I will either 6
be food for it or bring it for food to thee. Thy conceit is 7
nearer death than thy powers. For my sake be comfort- 8
able; hold death awhile at the arm's end. I will here be
with thee presently, and if I bring thee not something
to eat, I will give thee leave to die; but if thou diest
before I come, thou art a mocker of my labor. Well said;
thou look'st cheerily, and I'll be with thee quickly. Yet
thou liest in the bleak air. Come, I will bear thee to some
shelter, and thou shalt not die for lack of a dinner if
there live anything in this desert. Cheerily, good Adam.
                                              Exeunt.

*

Enter Duke Senior, and Lords, like Outlaws.   II, vii

DUKE SENIOR
I think he be transformed into a beast,
For I can nowhere find him like a man.

1. LORD
My lord, he is but even now gone hence;
Here was he merry, hearing of a song.

II, vi The Forest 6 *uncouth* uncivilized 7 *conceit* thought 8 *comfortable* cheerful
II, vii The Forest

DUKE SENIOR

5 If he, compact of jars, grow musical,
6 We shall have shortly discord in the spheres.
   Go seek him; tell him I would speak with him.
            Enter Jaques.

1. LORD

   He saves my labor by his own approach.

DUKE SENIOR

   Why, how now, monsieur, what a life is this,
   That your poor friends must woo your company?
   What, you look merrily.

JAQUES

   A fool, a fool! I met a fool i' th' forest,
13 A motley fool! a miserable world!
   As I do live by food, I met a fool
   Who laid him down and basked him in the sun
   And railed on Lady Fortune in good terms,
   In good set terms, and yet a motley fool.
   'Good morrow, fool,' quoth I. 'No, sir,' quoth he,
   'Call me not fool till heaven hath sent me fortune.'
20 And then he drew a dial from his poke,
   And looking on it with lack-lustre eye,
   Says very wisely, 'It is ten o'clock.
   Thus we may see,' quoth he, 'how the world wags.
   'Tis but an hour ago since it was nine,
   And after one hour more 'twill be eleven;
26 And so, from hour to hour, we ripe and ripe,
   And then, from hour to hour, we rot and rot;
   And thereby hangs a tale.' When I did hear
29 The motley fool thus moral on the time,
30 My lungs began to crow like chanticleer
   That fools should be so deep contemplative;

---

5 *compact of jars* composed of discords   **6** *spheres* (the harmonious crystal spheres in which the planets were supposedly set)   **13** *motley* wearing a costume of mixed colors, the conventional dress of a professional jester   **20** *dial* portable sundial; *poke* pocket   **26** *hour to hour* (perhaps a homonymic pun on 'whore')   **29** *moral* moralize   **30** *crow like chanticleer* exclaim triumphantly, like the crowing of the cock

And I did laugh sans intermission   32
An hour by his dial. O noble fool,
A worthy fool! Motley 's the only wear.   34

DUKE SENIOR
What fool is this?

JAQUES
O worthy fool! One that hath been a courtier,
And says, if ladies be but young and fair,
They have the gift to know it. And in his brain,
Which is as dry as the remainder biscuit   39
After a voyage, he hath strange places crammed
With observation, the which he vents
In mangled forms. O that I were a fool!
I am ambitious for a motley coat.

DUKE SENIOR
Thou shalt have one.

JAQUES   It is my only suit,   44
Provided that you weed your better judgments
Of all opinion that grows rank in them
That I am wise. I must have liberty
Withal, as large a charter as the wind,   48
To blow on whom I please, for so fools have.
And they that are most gallèd with my folly,   50
They most must laugh. And why, sir, must they so?
The why is plain as way to parish church:
He that a fool doth very wisely hit
Doth very foolishly, although he smart
Within, seem senseless of the bob. If not,   55
The wise man's folly is anatomized   56
Even by the squand'ring glances of the fool.   57
Invest me in my motley, give me leave
To speak my mind, and I will through and through

---

32 *sans* without   34 *wear* costume   39 *dry* (a dry brain was supposedly retentive)   44 *suit* (1) costume, (2) request   48 *large a charter* broad license   50 *gallèd* rubbed on a sore spot   55 *senseless of the bob* unaware of the taunt; *If not* if he does not acknowledge the hit   56 *anatomized* revealed, as by dissection   57 *squand'ring glances* random hits

Cleanse the foul body of th' infected world,
If they will patiently receive my medicine.

DUKE SENIOR

Fie on thee! I can tell what thou wouldst do.

JAQUES

63   What, for a counter, would I do but good?

DUKE SENIOR

Most mischievous foul sin, in chiding sin.
For thou thyself hast been a libertine,
66   As sensual as the brutish sting itself;
67   And all th' embossèd sores and headed evils
68   That thou with license of free foot hast caught,
Wouldst thou disgorge into the general world.

JAQUES

Why, who cries out on pride
71   That can therein tax any private party?
Doth it not flow as hugely as the sea
73   Till that the weary very means do ebb?
What woman in the city do I name
When that I say the city woman bears
The cost of princes on unworthy shoulders?
Who can come in and say that I mean her,
When such a one as she, such is her neighbor?
79   Or what is he of basest function
80   That says his bravery is not on my cost,
81   Thinking that I mean him, but therein suits
His folly to the mettle of my speech?
There then, how then, what then? Let me see wherein
My tongue hath wronged him. If it do him right,
85   Then he hath wronged himself. If he be free,
Why, then my taxing like a wild goose flies

---

63 *counter* worthless coin   66 *brutish sting* carnal appetite   67 *embossèd* swollen (the image here is from venereal disease)   68 *license . . . foot* licentious freedom   71 *tax* censure   73 *weary . . . ebb* i.e. ostentation subsides from exhaustion   79 *function* position in society   80 *says . . . cost* says his finery is not bought at my price, i.e. denies my criticism   81–82 *therein . . . speech* thus matches his folly with the substance of my remarks   85 *free* i.e. from blame

Unclaimed of any man. But who comes here?
Enter Orlando [with his sword drawn].

ORLANDO
Forbear, and eat no more!

JAQUES   Why, I have eat none yet.

ORLANDO
Nor shalt not, till necessity be served.

JAQUES
Of what kind should this cock come of?

DUKE SENIOR
Art thou thus boldened, man, by thy distress,
Or else a rude despiser of good manners,
That in civility thou seem'st so empty?

ORLANDO
You touched my vein at first. The thorny point   94
Of bare distress hath ta'en from me the show
Of smooth civility; yet am I inland bred   96
And know some nurture. But forbear, I say!   97
He dies that touches any of this fruit
Till I and my affairs are answerèd.   99

JAQUES
An you will not be answered with reason, I must die. 100

DUKE SENIOR
What would you have? Your gentleness shall force
More than your force move us to gentleness.

ORLANDO
I almost die for food, and let me have it!

DUKE SENIOR
Sit down and feed, and welcome to our table.

ORLANDO
Speak you so gently? Pardon me, I pray you.
I thought that all things had been savage here,
And therefore put I on the countenance   108

94 *vein* condition   96 *inland bred* raised in civilized society   97 *nurture*
proper upbringing   99 *answerèd* given attention   100 *An* if; *reason* (perhaps a homonymic pun on 'raisin,' i.e. grape, as Jaques takes fruit from the
table)   108 *countenance* appearance

Of stern commandment. But whate'er you are
That in this desert inaccessible,
Under the shade of melancholy boughs,
Lose and neglect the creeping hours of time ;
If ever you have looked on better days,
114   If ever been where bells have knolled to church,
If ever sat at any good man's feast,
If ever from your eyelids wiped a tear
And know what 'tis to pity and be pitied,
118   Let gentleness my strong enforcement be ;
119   In the which hope I blush, and hide my sword.

DUKE SENIOR
True is it that we have seen better days,
And have with holy bell been knolled to church,
And sat at good men's feasts, and wiped our eyes
Of drops that sacred pity hath engend'red ;
And therefore sit you down in gentleness,
125   And take upon command what help we have
That to your wanting may be minist'red.

ORLANDO
Then but forbear your food a little while,
Whiles, like a doe, I go to find my fawn
And give it food. There is an old poor man
Who after me hath many a weary step
Limped in pure love. Till he be first sufficed,
Oppressed with two weak evils, age and hunger,
I will not touch a bit.

DUKE SENIOR   Go find him out,
And we will nothing waste till you return.

ORLANDO
I thank ye, and be blest for your good comfort !   *[Exit.]*

DUKE SENIOR
Thou seest we are not all alone unhappy :
This wide and universal theatre

---

114 *knolled* called by chimes   118 *enforcement* inducement   119 *blush*
(original sense 'glow')   125 *upon command* for the asking

Presents more woeful pageants than the scene
Wherein we play in.
JAQUES   All the world's a stage,   139
And all the men and women merely players;
They have their exits and their entrances,
And one man in his time plays many parts,
His acts being seven ages. At first, the infant,
Mewling and puking in the nurse's arms.   144
Then the whining schoolboy, with his satchel
And shining morning face, creeping like snail
Unwillingly to school. And then the lover,
Sighing like furnace, with a woeful ballad
Made to his mistress' eyebrow. Then a soldier,
Full of strange oaths and bearded like the pard,   150
Jealous in honor, sudden and quick in quarrel,   151
Seeking the bubble reputation
Even in the cannon's mouth. And then the justice,
In fair round belly with good capon lined,   154
With eyes severe and beard of formal cut,
Full of wise saws and modern instances;   156
And so he plays his part. The sixth age shifts
Into the lean and slippered pantaloon,   158
With spectacles on nose and pouch on side;
His youthful hose, well saved, a world too wide
For his shrunk shank, and his big manly voice,
Turning again toward childish treble, pipes
And whistles in his sound. Last scene of all,   163
That ends this strange eventful history,
Is second childishness and mere oblivion,
Sans teeth, sans eyes, sans taste, sans everything.   166
    Enter Orlando, with Adam.

139 *All . . . stage* (a stock metaphor in classical and Renaissance literature, here given fresh vividness)   144 *Mewling* crying; *puking* vomiting   150 *pard* leopard   151 *Jealous in* zealous in seeking; *sudden* rash   154 *capon* (alluding to the well-known Elizabethan practice of offering a gift of a capon to a judge, in hope of gaining his favor)   156 *saws* maxims; *modern instances* everyday examples   158 *pantaloon* ridiculous old man (a figure in Italian comedy)   163 *his* its   166 s.d. *Enter . . . Adam* (see Introduction)

DUKE SENIOR
Welcome. Set down your venerable burden
And let him feed.

ORLANDO
I thank you most for him.

ADAM   So had you need.
I scarce can speak to thank you for myself.

DUKE SENIOR
Welcome, fall to. I will not trouble you
As yet to question you about your fortunes.
Give us some music ; and, good cousin, sing.

Song.

[AMIENS] Blow, blow, thou winter wind,
                Thou art not so unkind
                    As man's ingratitude :
                Thy tooth is not so keen,
178   Because thou art not seen,
                    Although thy breath be rude.
        Heigh-ho, sing heigh-ho, unto the green holly.
181   Most friendship is faining, most loving mere folly :
                Then, heigh-ho, the holly.
                This life is most jolly.

                Freeze, freeze, thou bitter sky
                That dost not bite so nigh
                    As benefits forgot :
187   Though thou the waters warp,
                Thy sting is not so sharp
                    As friend rememb'red not.
        Heigh-ho, sing, &c.

DUKE SENIOR
If that you were the good Sir Rowland's son,
As you have whispered faithfully you were,
193   And as mine eye doth his effigies witness

178 *not seen* (hence, not personal)   181 *faining* longing, wishful thinking
187 *warp* freeze   193 *effigies* replica (accent on second syllable)

Most truly limned and living in your face,   194
Be truly welcome hither. I am the Duke
That loved your father. The residue of your fortune
Go to my cave and tell me. Good old man,   197
Thou art right welcome, as thy master is.
Support him by the arm. Give me your hand,
And let me all your fortunes understand.   *Exeunt.*

❋

Enter Duke [Frederick], Lords, and Oliver.   III, i

DUKE FREDERICK
Not see him since? Sir, sir, that cannot be.
But were I not the better part made mercy,
I should not seek an absent argument   3
Of my revenge, thou present. But look to it :   4
Find out thy brother, wheresoe'er he is ;
Seek him with candle ; bring him dead or living
Within this twelvemonth, or turn thou no more   7
To seek a living in our territory.
Thy lands, and all things that thou dost call thine
Worth seizure, do we seize into our hands
Till thou canst quit thee by thy brother's mouth   11
Of what we think against thee.

OLIVER
O that your Highness knew my heart in this !
I never loved my brother in my life.

DUKE FREDERICK
More villain thou. Well, push him out of doors,
And let my officers of such a nature
Make an extent upon his house and lands.   17
Do this expediently and turn him going.   *Exeunt.*

❋

194 *limned* portrayed   197 *Go* walk
III, i Within Duke Frederick's palace   3 *argument* subject, i.e. Orlando
4 *thou present* you being present   7 *turn* return   11 *quit* acquit   17 *Make
...upon* seize by writ

III, ii   *Enter Orlando [, with a writing].*

ORLANDO
Hang there, my verse, in witness of my love;
2   And thou, thrice-crownèd Queen of Night, survey
With thy chaste eye, from thy pale sphere above,
4   Thy huntress' name that my full life doth sway.
O Rosalind! these trees shall be my books,
6   And in their barks my thoughts I'll character,
That every eye which in this forest looks
8   Shall see thy virtue witnessed everywhere.
Run, run, Orlando, carve on every tree
10   The fair, the chaste, and unexpressive she.   *Exit.*
          Enter Corin and [Touchstone the] Clown.

CORIN And how like you this shepherd's life, Master
Touchstone?

13 TOUCHSTONE Truly, shepherd, in respect of itself, it is a
good life; but in respect that it is a shepherd's life, it is
naught. In respect that it is solitary, I like it very well;
16   but in respect that it is private, it is a very vile life. Now
in respect it is in the fields, it pleaseth me well; but in
respect it is not in the court, it is tedious. As it is a spare
19   life, look you, it fits my humor well; but as there is no
more plenty in it, it goes much against my stomach.
Hast any philosophy in thee, shepherd?

CORIN No more but that I know the more one sickens the
worse at ease he is; and that he that wants money,
means, and content is without three good friends; that
the property of rain is to wet and fire to burn; that good
pasture makes fat sheep, and that a great cause of the
night is lack of the sun; that he that hath learned no wit
28   by nature nor art may complain of good breeding, or

III, ii The Forest of Arden   2 *thrice-crownèd . . . Night* the moon (the
triple crowning probably refers to the three goddesses associated with
the moon: Cynthia, Diana, Proserpina) · 4 *Thy huntress' name* (Rosalind
is conceived as a chaste huntress waiting on Diana)   6 *character* inscribe
8 *virtue* excellence   10 *unexpressive* beyond expression   13 *in respect of*
considering   16 *private* lonely   19 *humor* state of mind   28 *complain of*
decry the lack of

comes of a very dull kindred.

TOUCHSTONE Such a one is a natural philosopher. Wast ever in court, shepherd?

CORIN No, truly.

TOUCHSTONE Then thou art damned.

CORIN Nay, I hope.

TOUCHSTONE Truly thou art damned, like an ill-roasted egg, all on one side.

CORIN For not being at court? Your reason.

TOUCHSTONE Why, if thou never wast at court, thou never saw'st good manners; if thou never saw'st good manners, then thy manners must be wicked; and 39 wickedness is sin, and sin is damnation. Thou art in a parlous state, shepherd. 41

CORIN Not a whit, Touchstone. Those that are good manners at the court are as ridiculous in the country as the behavior of the country is most mockable at the court. You told me you salute not at the court but you 46 kiss your hands. That courtesy would be uncleanly if courtiers were shepherds.

TOUCHSTONE Instance, briefly; come, instance. 49

CORIN Why, we are still handling our ewes, and their 50 fells you know are greasy. 51

TOUCHSTONE Why, do not your courtier's hands sweat? and is not the grease of a mutton as wholesome as the sweat of a man? Shallow, shallow. A better instance, I say; come.

CORIN Besides, our hands are hard.

TOUCHSTONE Your lips will feel them the sooner. Shallow again. A more sounder instance, come.

CORIN And they are often tarred over with the surgery of 59 our sheep, and would you have us kiss tar? The courtier's hands are perfumed with civet.

---

39 *manners* (Touchstone plays on the meanings 'etiquette' and 'morals')
41 *parlous* perilous   46 *but* unless   49 *Instance* proof   50 *still* continually
51 *fells* fleeces   59 *tarred . . . surgery* covered with the tar used as ointment for sores

62 TOUCHSTONE Most shallow man! Thou worms' meat in respect of a good piece of flesh indeed! Learn of the wise,
64 and perpend. Civet is of a baser birth than tar, the very
65 uncleanly flux of a cat. Mend the instance, shepherd.

CORIN You have too courtly a wit for me; I'll rest.

TOUCHSTONE Wilt thou rest damned? God help thee,
68 shallow man! God make incision in thee! thou art raw.

CORIN Sir, I am a true laborer; I earn that I eat, get that I wear, owe no man hate, envy no man's happiness, glad of other men's good, content with my harm; and the greatest of my pride is to see my ewes graze and my lambs suck.

TOUCHSTONE That is another simple sin in you: to bring the ewes and the rams together and to offer to get your living by the copulation of cattle, to be bawd to a bell-wether and to betray a she-lamb of a twelvemonth to a
78 crookèd-pated old cuckoldly ram, out of all reasonable match. If thou beest not damned for this, the devil himself will have no shepherds; I cannot see else how thou shouldst 'scape.

CORIN Here comes young Master Ganymede, my new mistress's brother.

Enter Rosalind [, with a writing].

ROSALIND *[reads]*

  'From the east to western Inde,
  No jewel is like Rosalinde.
  Her worth, being mounted on the wind,
  Through all the world bears Rosalinde.
87   All the pictures fairest lined
  Are but black to Rosalinde.
  Let no face be kept in mind
  But the fair of Rosalinde.'

---

62 *worms' meat* food for worms, moribund flesh 64 *perpend* consider
65 *flux* secretion 68 *make incision in* operate on; *raw* crude (with play on 'sore,' requiring operation) 78 *crookèd-pated* with crooked horns; *cuckoldly* i.e. because he has horns 87 *lined* outlined, drawn

TOUCHSTONE I'll rhyme you so eight years together, dinners and suppers and sleeping hours excepted. It is 92 the right butterwomen's rank to market.

ROSALIND Out, fool!

TOUCHSTONE For a taste:

> If a hart do lack a hind,
> Let him seek out Rosalinde.
> If the cat will after kind,
> So be sure will Rosalinde.
> Wintred garments must be lined, 100
> So must slender Rosalinde.
> They that reap must sheaf and bind,
> Then to cart with Rosalinde. 103
> Sweetest nut hath sourest rind,
> Such a nut is Rosalinde.
> He that sweetest rose will find
> Must find love's prick, and Rosalinde.

This is the very false gallop of verses. Why do you infect 108 yourself with them?

ROSALIND Peace, you dull fool! I found them on a tree.

TOUCHSTONE Truly the tree yields bad fruit.

ROSALIND I'll graff it with you and then I shall graff it 112 with a medlar. Then it will be the earliest fruit i' th' 113 country; for you'll be rotten ere you be half ripe, and that's the right virtue of the medlar.

TOUCHSTONE You have said; but whether wisely or no, let the forest judge.

Enter Celia, with a writing.

ROSALIND Peace! Here comes my sister reading; stand aside.

92–93 *It is ... market* i.e. the verses jog on monotonously like farm women riding to market　100 *Wintred* prepared for winter　103 *to cart* (female delinquents were publicly carted through the streets)　108 *false gallop* gallop starting on wrong foot　112 *graff* graft　113 *medlar* a kind of pear not ready to eat until it starts to decay (with pun on 'meddler')

CELIA 'Why should this a desert be?
    For it is unpeopled? No.
    Tongues I'll hang on every tree
122   That shall civil sayings show:
    Some, how brief the life of man
    Runs his erring pilgrimage,
125   That the stretching of a span
126   Buckles in his sum of age;
    Some, of violated vows
    'Twixt the souls of friend and friend;
    But upon the fairest boughs,
    Or at every sentence end,
    Will I "Rosalinda" write,
    Teaching all that read to know
133   The quintessence of every sprite
134   Heaven would in little show.
    Therefore heaven Nature charged
    That one body should be filled
    With all graces wide-enlarged.
    Nature presently distilled
139   Helen's cheek, but not her heart,
    Cleopatra's majesty,
141   Atalanta's better part,
    Sad Lucretia's modesty.
    Thus Rosalinde of many parts
    By heavenly synod was devised,
    Of many faces, eyes, and hearts,
146   To have the touches dearest prized.
   Heaven would that she these gifts should have,
   And I to live and die her slave.'
149 ROSALIND O most gentle Jupiter, what tedious homily of
   love have you wearied your parishioners withal, and

---

122 *civil sayings* civilized comments 125 *stretching of a span* breadth of an open hand 126 *Buckles in* encompasses 133 *quintessence* pure essence (accent on first syllable); *sprite* spirit 134 *in little* i.e. in one person, the microcosm 139 *cheek* beauty; *heart* i.e. false heart 141 *Atalanta's better part* i.e. her beauty and swiftness, as opposed to her cruelty 146 *touches* features 149 *Jupiter* (frequently emended to 'pulpiter')

never cried, 'Have patience, good people'!

CELIA How now? Back, friends. Shepherd, go off a little.
Go with him, sirrah.

TOUCHSTONE Come, shepherd, let us make an honorable retreat; though not with bag and baggage, yet with
scrip and scrippage.   *Exit [with Corin].* 156

CELIA Didst thou hear these verses?

ROSALIND O, yes, I heard them all, and more too; for
some of them had in them more feet than the verses
would bear.

CELIA That's no matter. The feet might bear the verses.

ROSALIND Ay, but the feet were lame, and could not
bear themselves without the verse, and therefore stood
lamely in the verse.

CELIA But didst thou hear without wondering how thy
name should be hanged and carved upon these trees?

ROSALIND I was seven of the nine days out of the wonder 166
before you came; for look here what I found on a palm 167
tree. I was never so berhymed since Pythagoras' time 168
that I was an Irish rat, which I can hardly remember. 169

CELIA Trow you who hath done this?   170

ROSALIND Is it a man?

CELIA And a chain that you once wore, about his neck.
Change you color?

ROSALIND I prithee who?

CELIA O Lord, Lord, it is a hard matter for friends to
meet; but mountains may be removed with earth- 176
quakes, and so encounter.   177

ROSALIND Nay, but who is it?

CELIA Is it possible?

---

156 *scrip and scrippage* shepherd's pouch and its contents   166 *nine days* (a
reference to the common expression 'a nine days' wonder')   167 *palm*
(Lodge, in *Rosalynde*, mentions a palm tree in one of his euphuistic
aphorisms)   168 *Pythagoras* (to whom was attributed the doctrine of
transmigration of souls)   169 *Irish rat* (alluding to the belief that Irish
sorcerers could kill animals by means of rhymed spells)   170 *Trow you*
have you any idea   176 *removed with* moved by   177 *encounter* be brought
together

180 ROSALIND Nay, I prithee now with most petitionary vehemence, tell me who it is.

CELIA O wonderful, wonderful, and most wonderful
183 wonderful, and yet again wonderful, and after that, out of all hooping!

185 ROSALIND Good my complexion! Dost thou think,
186 though I am caparisoned like a man, I have a doublet
187 and hose in my disposition? One inch of delay more is a South Sea of discovery. I prithee tell me who is it quickly, and speak apace. I would thou couldst stammer, that thou mightst pour this concealed man out of thy mouth as wine comes out of a narrow-mouthed bottle; either too much at once, or none at all. I prithee take the cork out of thy mouth, that I may drink thy tidings.

CELIA So you may put a man in your belly.

195 ROSALIND Is he of God's making? What manner of man? Is his head worth a hat? or his chin worth a beard?

CELIA Nay, he hath but a little beard.

ROSALIND Why, God will send more, if the man will be thankful Let me stay the growth of his beard, if thou delay me not the knowledge of his chin.

CELIA It is young Orlando, that tripped up the wrestler's heels and your heart both in an instant.

203 ROSALIND Nay, but the devil take mocking! Speak sad brow and true maid.

CELIA I' faith, coz, 'tis he.

ROSALIND Orlando?

CELIA Orlando.

ROSALIND Alas the day! what shall I do with my doublet and hose? What did he when thou saw'st him? What
210 said he? How looked he? Wherein went he? What

180 *petitionary* suppliant   183–84 *out of all hooping* beyond all measure   185 *Good my complexion* O my (feminine) temperament   186 *caparisoned* bedecked (commonly used of horses)   187–88 *One . . . discovery* another minute of waiting will be as tedious as a journey to the South Seas for exploration   195 *of God's making* i.e. a real man, of flesh and blood   203–04 *sad . . . maid* seriously and truthfully   210 *Wherein went he* what did he wear

makes he here? Did he ask for me? Where remains he? 211
How parted he with thee? and when shalt thou see him
again? Answer me in one word.

CELIA You must borrow me Gargantua's mouth first; 214
'tis a word too great for any mouth of this age's size. To
say ay and no to these particulars is more than to answer
in a catechism.

ROSALIND But doth he know that I am in this forest,
and in man's apparel? Looks he as freshly as he did the
day he wrestled?

CELIA It is as easy to count atomies as to resolve the 221
propositions of a lover; but take a taste of my finding
him, and relish it with good observance. I found him 223
under a tree, like a dropped acorn.

ROSALIND It may well be called Jove's tree when it drops 225
such fruit.

CELIA Give me audience, good madam.

ROSALIND Proceed.

CELIA There lay he stretched along like a wounded
knight.

ROSALIND Though it be pity to see such a sight, it well
becomes the ground.   231

CELIA Cry 'holla' to thy tongue, I prithee; it curvets un- 232
seasonably. He was furnished like a hunter.

ROSALIND O, ominous! he comes to kill my heart.   234

CELIA I would sing my song without a burden. Thou 235
bring'st me out of tune.

ROSALIND Do you not know I am a woman? When I
think, I must speak. Sweet, say on.

Enter Orlando and Jaques.

CELIA You bring me out. Soft. Comes he not here?

ROSALIND 'Tis he! Slink by, and note him.

211 *makes* does **214** *Gargantua's mouth* (Rabelais' giant swallowed five
pilgrims in a salad) **221** *atomies* motes **221–22** *resolve the propositions*
answer the questions **223** *relish it* heighten it with sauce; *observance*
attention **225** *Jove's tree* (the oak was sacred to Jupiter) **231** *becomes*
adorns **232** *holla* halt; *curvets* prances **234** *heart* (quibble on 'hart')
235 *burden* undersong, refrain

JAQUES I thank you for your company; but, good faith, I
had as lief have been myself alone.

ORLANDO And so had I; but yet for fashion sake I thank
you too for your society.

JAQUES God b' wi' you; let's meet as little as we can.

ORLANDO I do desire we may be better strangers.

JAQUES I pray you mar no more trees with writing love
songs in their barks.

249 ORLANDO I pray you mar no moe of my verses with
250 reading them ill-favoredly.

JAQUES Rosalind is your love's name?

ORLANDO Yes, just.

JAQUES I do not like her name.

ORLANDO There was no thought of pleasing you when
she was christened.

JAQUES What stature is she of?

ORLANDO Just as high as my heart.

JAQUES You are full of pretty answers. Have you not
259 been acquainted with goldsmiths' wives, and conned
them out of rings?

261 ORLANDO Not so; but I answer you right painted cloth,
from whence you have studied your questions.

263 JAQUES You have a nimble wit; I think 'twas made of Atalanta's heels. Will you sit down with me? and we
two will rail against our mistress the world and all our
misery.

267 ORLANDO I will chide no breather in the world but myself, against whom I know most faults.

JAQUES The worst fault you have is to be in love.

ORLANDO 'Tis a fault I will not change for your best
virtue. I am weary of you.

---

249 *moe* more **250** *ill-favoredly* badly **259–60** *conned . . . rings* memorized
them from the verses engraved in rings **261** *right painted cloth* cheap
substitute tapestries, with painted pictures and mottoes **263–64** *Atalanta's
heels* (Atalanta was speedy enough to outrun her suitors) **267** *breather*
living creature

JAQUES By my troth, I was seeking for a fool when I found you.

ORLANDO He is drowned in the brook. Look but in and you shall see him.

JAQUES There I shall see mine own figure.

ORLANDO Which I take to be either a fool or a cipher.

JAQUES I'll tarry no longer with you. Farewell, good Signior Love.

ORLANDO I am glad of your departure. Adieu, good Monsieur Melancholy.   [Exit Jaques.]

ROSALIND I will speak to him like a saucy lackey, and under that habit play the knave with him. Do you hear, 283 forester?

ORLANDO Very well. What would you?

ROSALIND I pray you, what is't o'clock?

ORLANDO You should ask me, what time o' day. There's no clock in the forest.

ROSALIND Then there is no true lover in the forest, else sighing every minute and groaning every hour would detect the lazy foot of Time as well as a clock. 291

ORLANDO And why not the swift foot of Time? Had not that been as proper?

ROSALIND By no means, sir. Time travels in divers paces with divers persons. I'll tell you who Time ambles withal, who Time trots withal, who Time gallops 295 withal, and who he stands still withal.

ORLANDO I prithee, who doth he trot withal?

ROSALIND Marry, he trots hard with a young maid between the contract of her marriage and the day it is solemnized. If the interim be but a se'nnight, Time's 301 pace is so hard that it seems the length of seven year.

ORLANDO Who ambles Time withal?

ROSALIND With a priest that lacks Latin and a rich man that hath not the gout; for the one sleeps easily because

283 *habit* garb   291 *detect* call attention to   295 *withal* with you   301 *se'nnight* week

he cannot study, and the other lives merrily because he feels no pain; the one lacking the burden of lean and
307   wasteful learning, the other knowing no burden of heavy tedious penury. These Time ambles withal.

ORLANDO Who doth he gallop withal?

ROSALIND With a thief to the gallows; for though he go
312   as softly as foot can fall, he thinks himself too soon there.

ORLANDO Who stays it still withal?

ROSALIND With lawyers in the vacation; for they sleep
315   between term and term, and then they perceive not how time moves.

ORLANDO Where dwell you, pretty youth?

ROSALIND With this shepherdess, my sister; here in the skirts of the forest, like fringe upon a petticoat.

ORLANDO Are you native of this place?

321 ROSALIND As the cony that you see dwell where she is
322   kindled.

ORLANDO Your accent is something finer than you could
324   purchase in so removed a dwelling.

ROSALIND I have been told so of many. But indeed an old
326   religious uncle of mine taught me to speak, who was in
327   his youth an inland man; one that knew courtship too well, for there he fell in love. I have heard him read many lectures against it; and I thank God I am not a
330   woman, to be touched with so many giddy offenses as he hath generally taxed their whole sex withal.

ORLANDO Can you remember any of the principal evils that he laid to the charge of women?

ROSALIND There were none principal. They were all like one another as halfpence are, every one fault seeming monstrous till his fellow-fault came to match it.

ORLANDO I prithee recount some of them.

---

307 *wasteful* causing one to waste away   312 *softly* slowly   315 *term* court session   321 *cony* rabbit   322 *kindled* born   324 *purchase* acquire; *re-moved* remote   326 *religious* in holy orders   327 *inland* (see II, vii, 96n.); *courtship* (quibble on 'courtliness' and 'wooing')   330 *touched* tainted

ROSALIND No, I will not cast away my physic but on those that are sick. There is a man haunts the forest that abuses our young plants with carving 'Rosalind' on their barks, hangs odes upon hawthorns, and elegies on brambles; all, forsooth, deifying the name of Rosalind. If I could meet that fancy-monger, I would give him 343
some good counsel, for he seems to have the quotidian 344
of love upon him.

ORLANDO I am he that is so love-shaked. I pray you tell me your remedy.

ROSALIND There is none of my uncle's marks upon you. He taught me how to know a man in love; in which cage 349
of rushes I am sure you are not a prisoner.

ORLANDO What were his marks?

ROSALIND A lean cheek, which you have not; a blue eye 352
and sunken, which you have not; an unquestionable 353
spirit, which you have not; a beard neglected, which you have not: but I pardon you for that, for simply your 355
having in beard is a younger brother's revenue. Then your hose should be ungartered, your bonnet unbanded, your sleeve unbuttoned, your shoe untied, and everything about you demonstrating a careless desola-
tion. But you are no such man: you are rather point- 360
device in your accoustrements, as loving yourself than seeming the lover of any other.

ORLANDO Fair youth, I would I could make thee believe I love.

ROSALIND Me believe it? You may as soon make her that you love believe it, which I warrant she is apter to do than to confess she does; that is one of the points in the which women still give the lie to their consciences. But

---

343 *fancy-monger* i.e. one who advertises his so-called love 344 *quotidian* daily fever 349–50 *cage of rushes* flimsy prison (with a glancing allusion to the 'rush rings' used for mock marriages) 352 *blue eye* i.e. with dark circles 353 *unquestionable* unwilling to converse 355–56 *your having ... revenue* you have only a small portion of a beard 360–61 *point-device ... accoustrements* dressed with exactness

in good sooth, are you he that hangs the verses on the trees wherein Rosalind is so admired?

ORLANDO I swear to thee, youth, by the white hand of Rosalind, I am that he, that unfortunate he.

ROSALIND But are you so much in love as your rhymes speak?

ORLANDO Neither rhyme nor reason can express how much.

ROSALIND Love is merely a madness, and, I tell you,
377   deserves as well a dark house and a whip as madmen do; and the reason why they are not so punished and cured is that the lunacy is so ordinary that the whippers are in love too. Yet I profess curing it by counsel.

ORLANDO Did you ever cure any so?

ROSALIND Yes, one, and in this manner. He was to imagine me his love, his mistress; and I set him every day to
384   woo me. At which time would I, being but a moonish youth, grieve, be effeminate, changeable, longing and liking, proud, fantastical, apish, shallow, inconstant, full of tears, full of smiles; for every passion something and for no passion truly anything, as boys and women are for the most part cattle of this color; would now like him, now loathe him; then entertain him, then forswear him; now weep for him, then spit at him; that I drave
392   my suitor from his mad humor of love to a living humor of madness, which was, to forswear the full stream of the world and to live in a nook merely monastic. And thus I cured him; and this way will I take upon me to wash
396   your liver as clean as a sound sheep's heart, that there shall not be one spot of love in't.

ORLANDO I would not be cured, youth.

ROSALIND I would cure you, if you would but call me
400   Rosalind and come every day to my cote and woo me.

---

377 *a dark . . . whip* (the shock treatment by which the Elizabethans attempted to cure insanity)   384 *moonish* fickle   392 *humor* state   396 *liver* (supposed to be the source of the passions, especially love)   400 *cote* cottage

ORLANDO Now, by the faith of my love, I will. Tell me
where it is.

ROSALIND Go with me to it, and I'll show it you; and by
the way you shall tell me where in the forest you live.
Will you go?

ORLANDO With all my heart, good youth.

ROSALIND Nay, you must call me Rosalind. Come,
sister, will you go?   *Exeunt.*

*

Enter [Touchstone the] Clown, Audrey; and Jaques   III, iii
[apart].

TOUCHSTONE Come apace, good Audrey. I will fetch up
your goats, Audrey. And how, Audrey, am I the man
yet? Doth my simple feature content you?   3

AUDREY Your features, Lord warrant us! What features?   4

TOUCHSTONE I am here with thee and thy goats, as the   5
most capricious poet, honest Ovid, was among the
Goths.

JAQUES *[aside]* O knowledge ill-inhabited, worse than   7
Jove in a thatched house!   8

TOUCHSTONE When a man's verses cannot be under-   9
stood, nor a man's good wit seconded with the forward
child, understanding, it strikes a man more dead than a   11
great reckoning in a little room. Truly, I would the gods
had made thee poetical.

AUDREY I do not know what poetical is. Is it honest in

III, iii The Forest   3 *simple feature* plain appearance   4 *features* (Audrey
evidently misunderstands Touchstone, but the nature of the joke is
obscure)   5–7 *goats . . . Goths* (Ovid was exiled among the Goths, here
pronounced 'goats.' Touchstone quibbles on 'goats' and 'capricious,' the
latter deriving from Latin '*caper*,' a male goat.)   7 *ill-inhabited* poorly
lodged   8 *Jove . . . house* (Jupiter, in human form, was once entertained
by two peasants in their thatched cottage)   9–11 *When . . . understanding*
i.e. Audrey has failed to appreciate Touchstone's wit, just as the Goths
failed to appreciate Ovid's poetry   11–12 *a great reckoning in* a large
bill for

deed and word? Is it a true thing?

16 TOUCHSTONE No, truly; for the truest poetry is the most faining, and lovers are given to poetry, and what they swear in poetry may be said, as lovers, they do feign.

AUDREY Do you wish then that the gods had made me poetical?

TOUCHSTONE I do truly; for thou swear'st to me thou art honest. Now if thou wert a poet, I might have some hope thou didst feign.

AUDREY Would you not have me honest?

25 TOUCHSTONE No, truly, unless thou wert hard-favored;
26 for honesty coupled to beauty is to have honey a sauce to sugar.

28 JAQUES [aside] A material fool.

AUDREY Well, I am not fair, and therefore I pray the gods make me honest.

TOUCHSTONE Truly, and to cast away honesty upon a foul slut were to put good meat into an unclean dish.

33 AUDREY I am not a slut, though I thank the gods I am foul.

TOUCHSTONE Well, praised be the gods for thy foulness! Sluttishness may come hereafter. But be it as it may be,
36 I will marry thee; and to that end I have been with Sir Oliver Mar-text, the vicar of the next village, who hath promised to meet me in this place of the forest and to couple us.

JAQUES [aside] I would fain see this meeting.

AUDREY Well, the gods give us joy!

TOUCHSTONE Amen. A man may, if he were of a fearful heart, stagger in this attempt; for here we have no temple

---

16–18 *truest poetry . . . feign* (Touchstone apparently has in mind here the first line of Sidney's *Astrophel and Stella*, 'Loving in truth, and fain in verse my love to show.' But through his puns on 'fain' (desire) and 'feign' (pretend) he is insinuating a carnal interpretation of 'poetic' love.) 25 *hard-favored* ugly 26 *honesty* chastity (a meaning latent in Touchstone's earlier use of *honest*) 28 *material* making good sense 33 *foul* (Audrey interprets the word as 'ugly') 36 *Sir* (an old-fashioned designation for a clergyman)

but the wood, no assembly but horn-beasts. But what 44
though? Courage! As horns are odious, they are necessary. It is said, 'Many a man knows no end of his goods.'
Right! Many a man has good horns and knows no end
of them. Well, that is the dowry of his wife; 'tis none of
his own getting. Horns. Even so, poor men alone. No,
no; the noblest deer hath them as huge as the rascal. Is 50
the single man therefore blessed? No; as a walled town
is more worthier than a village, so is the forehead of a
married man more honorable than the bare brow of a
bachelor; and by how much defense is better than no 54
skill, by so much is a horn more precious than to want. 55

    Enter Sir Oliver Mar-text.

Here comes Sir Oliver. Sir Oliver Mar-text, you are
well met. Will you dispatch us here under this tree, or 57
shall we go with you to your chapel?

OLIVER MAR-TEXT Is there none here to give the
woman?

TOUCHSTONE I will not take her on gift of any man.

OLIVER MAR-TEXT Truly, she must be given, or the
marriage is not lawful.

JAQUES *[comes forward]* Proceed, proceed; I'll give her.

TOUCHSTONE Good even, good Master What-ye-call't. 64
How do you, sir? You are very well met. Goddild you 65
for your last company; I am very glad to see you. Even a
toy in hand here, sir. Nay, pray be covered. 67

JAQUES Will you be married, motley?

TOUCHSTONE As the ox hath his bow, sir, the horse his 69
curb, and the falcon her bells, so man hath his desires;
and as pigeons bill, so wedlock would be nibbling.

---

44 *horn-beasts* (throughout this passage Touchstone plays on the old joke
that cuckolds, i.e. men whose wives play them false, sprout horns) 50 *rascal*
inferior deer 54 *defense* i.e. the art of defending oneself, probably fencing
55 *to want* i.e. to lack horns 57 *dispatch us* finish off our business 64
Master What-ye-call't (Touchstone calls attention to Jaques' name, which
suggests the Elizabethan word for a privy, 'jakes') 65 *Goddild* God yield,
i.e. reward 67 *toy* trifle 69 *bow* collar of the yoke

JAQUES And will you, being a man of your breeding, be
73   married under a bush like a beggar? Get you to church,
   and have a good priest that can tell you what marriage
75   is. This fellow will but join you together as they join
   wainscot; then one of you will prove a shrunk panel,
   and like green timber warp, warp.

TOUCHSTONE [aside] I am not in the mind but I were
   better to be married of him than of another; for he is not
   like to marry me well; and not being well married, it
   will be a good excuse for me hereafter to leave my wife.

JAQUES Go thou with me and let me counsel thee.

TOUCHSTONE Come, sweet Audrey. We must be mar-
84   ried, or we must live in bawdry. Fare well, good Master
   Oliver: not
86   O sweet Oliver,
             O brave Oliver,
          Leave me not behind thee;
   but
            Wind away,
            Be gone, I say;
          I will not to wedding with thee.
                Exeunt [Jaques, Touchstone, and Audrey].
93 OLIVER MAR-TEXT 'Tis no matter. Ne'er a fantastical
   knave of them all shall flout me out of my calling. [Exit.]

*

      Enter Rosalind and Celia.

ROSALIND Never talk to me; I will weep.

CELIA Do, I prithee; but yet have the grace to consider
   that tears do not become a man.

---

73 *married . . . bush* (Oliver is a 'hedge-priest,' i.e. uneducated, unable to
expound the obligations of marriage)   **75–76** *as . . . wainscot* i.e. as they set
panelling together, without mortising or joining securely   **84** *bawdry*
immorality   **86ff.** *O sweet Oliver . . .* (snatches from a current ballad)
93 *fantastical* affected
III, iv The Forest

ROSALIND But have I not cause to weep?

CELIA As good cause as one would desire; therefore weep.

ROSALIND His very hair is of the dissembling color. 6

CELIA Something browner than Judas's. Marry, his kisses are Judas's own children. 8

ROSALIND I' faith, his hair is of a good color.

CELIA An excellent color. Your chestnut was ever the only color.

ROSALIND And his kissing is as full of sanctity as the touch of holy bread.

CELIA He hath bought a pair of cast lips of Diana. A nun 14
of winter's sisterhood kisses not more religiously; the 15
very ice of chastity is in them.

ROSALIND But why did he swear he would come this morning, and comes not?

CELIA Nay, certainly there is no truth in him.

ROSALIND Do you think so?

CELIA Yes; I think he is not a pickpurse nor a horse-stealer, but for his verity in love, I do think him as concave as a covered goblet or a worm-eaten nut. 23

ROSALIND Not true in love?

CELIA Yes, when he is in, but I think he is not in.

ROSALIND You have heard him swear downright he was.

CELIA 'Was' is not 'is.' Besides, the oath of a lover is no stronger than the word of a tapster; they are both the confirmer of false reckonings. He attends here in the forest on the Duke your father.

ROSALIND I met the Duke yesterday and had much question with him. He asked me of what parentage I was. I told him, of as good as he; so he laughed and let me go. But what talk we of fathers when there is such a man as Orlando?

---

6 *dissembling color* i.e. reddish, the traditional color of Judas' hair **8**
Judas's own children i.e. offspring of a betrayer **14** *cast* (1) discarded, (2)
statuary; perhaps with a play on 'chaste' (Diana was the goddess of chastity)
15 *of winter's sisterhood* i.e. sworn to coldness **23** *concave* hollow

36 CELIA O, that's a brave man; he writes brave verses,
speaks brave words, swears brave oaths, and breaks
38   them bravely, quite traverse, athwart the heart of his
39   lover, as a puisny tilter, that spurs his horse but on one
40   side, breaks his staff like a noble goose. But all's brave
that youth mounts and folly guides. Who comes here?
          Enter Corin.

CORIN
Mistress and master, you have oft enquired
After the shepherd that complained of love,
Who you saw sitting by me on the turf,
Praising the proud disdainful shepherdess
That was his mistress.

CELIA   Well, and what of him?

CORIN
47   If you will see a pageant truly played
Between the pale complexion of true love
And the red glow of scorn and proud disdain,
Go hence a little, and I shall conduct you,
If you will mark it.

ROSALIND   O, come, let us remove:
The sight of lovers feedeth those in love.
Bring us to this sight, and you shall say
I'll prove a busy actor in their play.   *Exeunt.*

*

III, v   *Enter Silvius and Phebe.*

SILVIUS
Sweet Phebe, do not scorn me; do not, Phebe!
Say that you love me not, but say not so
In bitterness. The common executioner,

---

36 *brave* excellent   38 *traverse* (a term in tilting, for hitting an opponent
sideways, awkwardly, instead of head-on)   39 *puisny* puny, i.e. inferior
40 *noble goose* grand fool   47 *pageant* performance
III, v The Forest

Whose heart th'accustomed sight of death makes hard,
Falls not the axe upon the humbled neck   5
But first begs pardon. Will you sterner be
Than he that dies and lives by bloody drops?   7
      Enter [apart] Rosalind, Celia, and Corin.

PHEBE
   I would not be thy executioner.
   I fly thee, for I would not injure thee.
   Thou tell'st me there is murder in mine eye:
   'Tis pretty, sure, and very probable
   That eyes, that are the frail'st and softest things,
   Who shut their coward gates on atomies,   13
   Should be called tyrants, butchers, murderers.
   Now I do frown on thee with all my heart,
   And if mine eyes can wound, now let them kill thee.
   Now counterfeit to swound; why, now fall down;   17
   Or if thou canst not, O, for shame, for shame,
   Lie not, to say mine eyes are murderers.
   Now show the wound mine eye hath made in thee;
   Scratch thee but with a pin, and there remains
   Some scar of it; lean upon a rush,
   The cicatrice and capable impressure   23
   Thy palm some moment keeps; but now mine eyes,
   Which I have darted at thee, hurt thee not,
   Nor I am sure there is no force in eyes
   That can do hurt.
SILVIUS   O dear Phebe,
   If ever, as that ever may be near,
   You meet in some fresh cheek the power of fancy,   29
   Then shall you know the wounds invisible
   That love's keen arrows make.
PHEBE   But till that time
   Come thou not near me; and when that time comes,

---

5 *Falls* lets fall   **7** *dies and lives* makes his living   **13** *atomies* motes   **17**
counterfeit to swound pretend to swoon   **23** *cicatrice* mark (literally, scar);
capable impressure i.e. impression capable of being seen   **29** *fancy* love

Afflict me with thy mocks, pity me not,
As till that time I shall not pity thee.

ROSALIND

And why, I pray you? Who might be your mother,
That you insult, exult, and all at once,
Over the wretched? What though you have no beauty
(As, by my faith, I see no more in you
39   Than without candle may go dark to bed)
Must you be therefore proud and pitiless?
Why, what means this? Why do you look on me?
42   I see no more in you than in the ordinary
43   Of nature's sale-work. 'Od's my little life,
I think she means to tangle my eyes too!
No, faith, proud mistress, hope not after it;
'Tis not your inky brows, your black silk hair,
47   Your bugle eyeballs, nor your cheek of cream
That can entame my spirits to your worship.
You foolish shepherd, wherefore do you follow her,
50   Like foggy south, puffing with wind and rain?
51   You are a thousand times a properer man
Than she a woman. 'Tis such fools as you
That makes the world full of ill-favored children.
'Tis not her glass, but you, that flatters her,
And out of you she sees herself more proper
Than any of her lineaments can show her.
But mistress, know yourself. Down on your knees,
And thank heaven, fasting, for a good man's love;
For I must tell you friendly in your ear,
Sell when you can, you are not for all markets.
61   Cry the man mercy, love him, take his offer;
62   Foul is most foul, being foul to be a scoffer;
So take her to thee, shepherd. Fare you well.

---

39 *may . . . bed* i.e. she does not have the beauty which (metaphorically)
illuminates the dark   42 *ordinary* common run   43 *sale-work* ready-made
products, not distinctive   47 *bugle* glassy, with black center   50 *south*
south wind   51 *properer* more handsome   61 *Cry . . . mercy* beg the man's
pardon   62 *Foul is most foul* ugliness is most repulsive

PHEBE

    Sweet youth, I pray you chide a year together;
    I had rather hear you chide than this man woo.

ROSALIND *[aside]* He's fall'n in love with your foulness,
    and she'll fall in love with my anger. If it be so, as fast as
    she answers thee with frowning looks, I'll sauce her
    with bitter words. *[to Phebe]* Why look you so upon me?

PHEBE

    For no ill will I bear you.

ROSALIND

    I pray you do not fall in love with me,
    For I am falser than vows made in wine.
    Besides, I like you not. If you will know my house,
    'Tis at the tuft of olives, here hard by.
    Will you go, sister? Shepherd, ply her hard.
    Come, sister. Shepherdess, look on him better
    And be not proud. Though all the world could see,
    None could be so abused in sight as he.
    Come, to our flock.   *Exit [with Celia and Corin]*.

PHEBE

    Dead shepherd, now I find thy saw of might,   80
    'Who ever loved that loved not at first sight?'   81

SILVIUS

    Sweet Phebe.

PHEBE   Ha! what say'st thou, Silvius?

SILVIUS

    Sweet Phebe, pity me.

PHEBE

    Why, I am sorry for thee, gentle Silvius.

SILVIUS

    Wherever sorrow is, relief would be.
    If you do sorrow at my grief in love,
    By giving love your sorrow and my grief
    Were both extermined.   88

80 *Dead shepherd* Christopher Marlowe (here referred to as a pastoral poet), who was killed in 1593; *saw* saying 81 '*Who . . . sight*' (Marlowe's *Hero and Leander* [pub. 1598], I, 175) 88 *extermined* expunged

PHEBE

89   Thou hast my love. Is not that neighborly?

SILVIUS

I would have you.

PHEBE   Why, that were covetousness.
Silvius, the time was that I hated thee;
92   And yet it is not that I bear thee love,
But since that thou canst talk of love so well,
Thy company, which erst was irksome to me,
I will endure; and I'll employ thee too;
But do not look for further recompense
Than thine own gladness that thou art employed.

SILVIUS

So holy and so perfect is my love,
And I in such a poverty of grace,
That I shall think it a most plenteous crop
To glean the broken ears after the man
That the main harvest reaps. Loose now and then
A scatt'red smile, and that I'll live upon.

PHEBE

Know'st thou the youth that spoke to me erewhile?

SILVIUS

Not very well, but I have met him oft,
And he hath bought the cottage and the bounds
107   That the old carlot once was master of.

PHEBE

Think not I love him, though I ask for him;
'Tis but a peevish boy; yet he talks well.
But what care I for words? Yet words do well
When he that speaks them pleases those that hear.
It is a pretty youth; not very pretty;
But sure he's proud; and yet his pride becomes him.
He'll make a proper man. The best thing in him
Is his complexion; and faster than his tongue

---

89 *neighborly* (possibly a reference to the commandment 'Thou shalt love thy neighbor as thyself')   92 *it is not* the time has not come   107 *carlot* countryman

Did make offense, his eye did heal it up.
He is not very tall ; yet for his years he's tall.
His leg is but so so ; and yet 'tis well.
There was a pretty redness in his lip,
A little riper and more lusty red
Than that mixed in his cheek ; 'twas just the difference
Betwixt the constant red and mingled damask.   122
There be some women, Silvius, had they marked him
In parcels as I did, would have gone near   124
To fall in love with him ; but, for my part,
I love him not nor hate him not ; and yet
I have more cause to hate him than to love him ;
For what had he to do to chide at me ?
He said mine eyes were black and my hair black ;
And, now I am rememb'red, scorned at me.   130
I marvel why I answered not again.
But that's all one : omittance is no quittance.   132
I'll write to him a very taunting letter,
And thou shalt bear it. Wilt thou, Silvius ?

SILVIUS
Phebe, with all my heart.
PHEBE   I'll write it straight ;   135
The matter 's in my head and in my heart ;
I will be bitter with him and passing short.   137
Go with me, Silvius.   *Exeunt.*

                        ✳

Enter Rosalind and Celia and Jaques.   IV, i
JAQUES I prithee, pretty youth, let me be better acquain-
ted with thee.
ROSALIND They say you are a melancholy fellow.
JAQUES I am so ; I do love it better than laughing.

---

122 *mingled damask* pink and white, the colors of damask roses   124 *In parcels* part by part   130 *rememb'red* reminded   132 *omittance is no quittance* i.e. failure to assert one's rights is not renunciation of them   135 *straight* straightway   137 *passing short* extremely curt
IV, i The Forest

5 ROSALIND Those that are in extremity of either are
abominable fellows, and betray themselves to every
7 modern censure worse than drunkards.

JAQUES Why, 'tis good to be sad and say nothing.

ROSALIND Why then, 'tis good to be a post.

JAQUES I have neither the scholar's melancholy, which is
11 emulation; nor the musician's, which is fantastical; nor
the courtier's, which is proud; nor the soldier's, which
13 is ambitious; nor the lawyer's, which is politic; nor the
14 lady's, which is nice; nor the lover's, which is all these:
but it is a melancholy of mine own, compounded of
16 many simples, extracted from many objects, and indeed
17 the sundry contemplation of my travels, which, by often
18 rumination, wraps me in a most humorous sadness.

ROSALIND A traveller! By my faith, you have great
reason to be sad. I fear you have sold your own lands to
see other men's. Then to have seen much and to have
nothing is to have rich eyes and poor hands.

JAQUES Yes, I have gained my experience.

Enter Orlando.

ROSALIND And your experience makes you sad. I had
rather have a fool to make me merry than experience
26 to make me sad: and to travel for it too.

ORLANDO Good day and happiness, dear Rosalind.

JAQUES Nay then, God b' wi' you, an you talk in blank
verse.

30 ROSALIND Farewell, Monsieur Traveller. Look you lisp
31 and wear strange suits, disable all the benefits of your
32 own country, be out of love with your nativity, and almost chide God for making you that countenance you
34 are; or I will scarce think you have swam in a gundello.
[Exit Jaques.]

5 *are in extremity* go to extremes   7 *modern* common   11 *emulation* envy;
fantastical absurdly elaborate   13 *politic* a matter of policy (to appear
learned)   14 *nice* over-refined   16 *simples* ingredients   17 *sundry* collected   18 *humorous* moody   26 *travel* (pun on 'travail,' i.e. labor)   30
lisp i.e. use foreign sounds   31 *disable* disparage   32 *nativity* birthplace
34 *swam in a gundello* i.e. been to Venice, to ride in a gondola

Why, how now, Orlando, where have you been all this
while? You a lover? An you serve me such another
trick, never come in my sight more.

ORLANDO My fair Rosalind, I come within an hour of my
promise.

ROSALIND Break an hour's promise in love? He that will
divide a minute into a thousand parts and break but a
part of the thousand part of a minute in the affairs of
love, it may be said of him that Cupid hath clapped him 43
o' th' shoulder, but I'll warrant him heart-whole.

ORLANDO Pardon me, dear Rosalind.

ROSALIND Nay, an you be so tardy, come no more in my
sight. I had as lief be wooed of a snail.

ORLANDO Of a snail?

ROSALIND Ay, of a snail; for though he comes slowly, he
carries his house on his head; a better jointure, I think, 50
than you make a woman. Besides, he brings his destiny
with him.

ORLANDO What's that?

ROSALIND Why, horns; which such as you are fain to be
beholding to your wives for; but he comes armed in his
fortune and prevents the slander of his wife. 56

ORLANDO Virtue is no horn-maker, and my Rosalind is
virtuous.

ROSALIND And I am your Rosalind.

CELIA It pleases him to call you so; but he hath a Rosalind
of a better leer than you. 61

ROSALIND Come, woo me, woo me; for now I am in a
holiday humor and like enough to consent. What would
you say to me now, and I were your very very Rosalind?

ORLANDO I would kiss before I spoke.

ROSALIND Nay, you were better speak first, and when you
were gravelled for lack of matter, you might take occa- 67
sion to kiss. Very good orators, when they are out, they 68

43–44 *clapped him o' th' shoulder* accosted him 50 *jointure* marriage
settlement 56 *prevents* forestalls 61 *leer* look 67 *gravelled* stuck 68
out out of matter

69   will spit; and for lovers, lacking – God warn us! –
matter, the cleanliest shift is to kiss.

ORLANDO How if the kiss be denied?

ROSALIND Then she puts you to entreaty, and there
begins new matter.

ORLANDO Who could be out, being before his beloved
mistress?

ROSALIND Marry, that should you, if I were your mis-
77   tress, or I should think my honesty ranker than my wit.

78 ORLANDO What, of my suit?

ROSALIND Not out of your apparel, and yet out of your
suit. Am not I your Rosalind?

ORLANDO I take some joy to say you are, because I would
be talking of her.

ROSALIND Well, in her person, I say I will not have you.

ORLANDO Then, in mine own person, I die.

85 ROSALIND No, faith, die by attorney. The poor world is
almost six thousand years old, and in all this time there
87   was not any man died in his own person, videlicet, in a
88   love cause. Troilus had his brains dashed out with a
Grecian club; yet he did what he could to die before,
90   and he is one of the patterns of love. Leander, he would
have lived many a fair year though Hero had turned
nun, if it had not been for a hot midsummer night; for,
good youth, he went but forth to wash him in the
Hellespont, and being taken with the cramp, was
95   drowned; and the foolish chroniclers of that age found
it was 'Hero of Sestos.' But these are all lies. Men have
died from time to time, and worms have eaten them,
but not for love.

---

69 *warn* save   77 *honesty* chastity; *ranker* less pure   78 *suit* plea (but Rosalind in reply puns on the word)   85 *by attorney* by proxy   87 *videlicet* namely   88 *Troilus* the faithful lover of the faithless Cressida in Chaucer's *Troilus and Criseyde* and earlier legends   88–89 *brains . . . club* (Rosalind's fiction is a travesty on Troilus)   90 *Leander* the faithful lover in classical myth and Marlowe's *Hero and Leander* (whose death Rosalind also travesties)   95–96 *foolish chroniclers . . . Sestos* the dimwitted storytellers decided he died for love of Hero, the lady of Sestos

ORLANDO I would not have my right Rosalind of this mind, for I protest her frown might kill me.

ROSALIND By this hand, it will not kill a fly. But come, now I will be your Rosalind in a more coming-on 102 disposition; and ask me what you will, I will grant it.

ORLANDO Then love me, Rosalind.

ROSALIND Yes, faith, will I, Fridays and Saturdays and all.

ORLANDO And wilt thou have me?

ROSALIND Ay, and twenty such.

ORLANDO What sayest thou?

ROSALIND Are you not good?

ORLANDO I hope so.

ROSALIND Why then, can one desire too much of a good thing? Come, sister, you shall be the priest and marry us. Give me your hand, Orlando. What do you say, sister?

ORLANDO Pray thee marry us.

CELIA I cannot say the words.

ROSALIND You must begin, 'Will you, Orlando' –

CELIA Go to. Will you, Orlando, have to wife this Rosa- 117 lind?

ORLANDO I will.

ROSALIND Ay, but when?

ORLANDO Why now, as fast as she can marry us.

ROSALIND Then you must say, 'I take thee, Rosalind, for wife.'

ORLANDO I take thee, Rosalind, for wife.

ROSALIND I might ask you for your commission; but I do 125 take thee, Orlando, for my husband. There's a girl goes 126 before the priest, and certainly a woman's thought runs before her actions.

ORLANDO So do all thoughts; they are winged.

ROSALIND Now tell me how long you would have her after you have possessed her.

102 *coming-on* yielding 117 *Go to* (equivalent to 'come now') 125 *commission* authority 126-27 *goes before* anticipates

ORLANDO For ever and a day.

ROSALIND Say 'a day,' without the 'ever.' No, no, Orlando; men are April when they woo, December when they
wed. Maids are May when they are maids, but the sky
changes when they are wives. I will be more jealous of
137   thee than a Barbary cock-pigeon over his hen, more
138   clamorous than a parrot against rain, more newfangled
than an ape, more giddy in my desires than a monkey.
140   I will weep for nothing, like Diana in the fountain, and
I will do that when you are disposed to be merry; I will
laugh like a hyen, and that when thou art inclined to sleep.

ORLANDO But will my Rosalind do so?

ROSALIND By my life, she will do as I do.

ORLANDO O, but she is wise.

ROSALIND Or else she could not have the wit to do this;
148   the wiser, the waywarder. Make the doors upon a
woman's wit, and it will out at the casement; shut that,
and 'twill out at the keyhole; stop that, 'twill fly with
the smoke out at the chimney.

ORLANDO A man that had a wife with such a wit, he
153   might say, 'Wit, whither wilt?'

154 ROSALIND Nay, you might keep that check for it till you
met your wife's wit going to your neighbor's bed.

ORLANDO And what wit could wit have to excuse that?

ROSALIND Marry, to say she came to seek you there. You
shall never take her without her answer unless you take
her without her tongue. O, that woman that cannot
160   make her fault her husband's occasion, let her never
161   nurse her child herself, for she will breed it like a fool.

---

137 *Barbary cock-pigeon* the 'Barb' pigeon, which originally came from the
north of Africa   138 *against* in anticipation of   140 *Diana in the fountain*
(Stow, in his *Survay of London*, 1603, reported that in 1596 at 'the great
Crosse in West Cheape' was 'set up . . . an Alablaster Image of Diana, and
water convayed from the Thames, prilling from her naked brest.' Rosalind
changes the figure to weeping.)   148 *Make* make fast   153 *wilt* will you go
154 *check* retort   160 *make . . . occasion* make her husband the cause of her
fault   161 *breed* raise

ORLANDO For these two hours, Rosalind, I will leave thee.

ROSALIND Alas, dear love, I cannot lack thee two hours!

ORLANDO I must attend the Duke at dinner. By two o'clock I will be with thee again.

ROSALIND Ay, go your ways, go your ways; I knew what you would prove. My friends told me as much, and I thought no less. That flattering tongue of yours won me. 'Tis but one cast away, and so, come death! Two o'clock is your hour?

ORLANDO Ay, sweet Rosalind.

ROSALIND By my troth, and in good earnest, and so God mend me, and by all pretty oaths that are not dangerous, if you break one jot of your promise or come one minute behind your hour, I will think you the most pathetical 176 break-promise, and the most hollow lover, and the most unworthy of her you call Rosalind, that may be chosen out of the gross band of the unfaithful. Therefore beware my censure and keep your promise.

ORLANDO With no less religion than if thou wert indeed 181 my Rosalind. So adieu.

ROSALIND Well, Time is the old justice that examines all such offenders, and let Time try. Adieu. *Exit [Orlando].*

CELIA You have simply misused our sex in your love-prate. We must have your doublet and hose plucked over your head, and show the world what the bird hath done to her own nest.

ROSALIND O coz, coz, coz, my pretty little coz, that thou didst know how many fathom deep I am in love! But it cannot be sounded. My affection hath an unknown bottom, like the Bay of Portugal.   192

CELIA Or rather, bottomless, that as fast as you pour affection in, it runs out.

ROSALIND No, that same wicked bastard of Venus that 195

---

176 *pathetical* pitiful   181 *With . . . religion* no less religiously   192 *Bay of Portugal* (the sea off the coast of Portugal was unplumbed)   195 *bastard of Venus* Cupid

196   was begot of thought, conceived of spleen, and born of
madness, that blind rascally boy that abuses every one's
eyes because his own are out, let him be judge how deep
I am in love. I'll tell thee, Aliena, I cannot be out of the
sight of Orlando. I'll go find a shadow, and sigh till he
come.

CELIA And I'll sleep.   *Exeunt.*

*

IV, ii   *Enter Jaques ; and Lords,[as] Foresters.*

JAQUES Which is he that killed the deer ?

[1.] LORD Sir, it was I.

JAQUES Let's present him to the Duke like a Roman con-
queror ; and it would do well to set the deer's horns
upon his head for a branch of victory. Have you no
song, forester, for this purpose ?

7 [2.] LORD Yes, sir.

JAQUES Sing it. 'Tis no matter how it be in tune, so it
make noise enough.

         Music.

                 Song.

What shall he have that killed the deer ?
His leather skin and horns to wear :

12   Then sing him home. *(The rest shall bear this burden.)*
Take thou no scorn to wear the horn,
It was a crest ere thou wast born,
    Thy father's father wore it,
    And thy father bore it.
The horn, the horn, the lusty horn,
Is not a thing to laugh to scorn.   *Exeunt.*

*

196 *thought* i.e. fancy; *spleen* impulse
IV, ii The Forest   7 *[2.] Lord* (speech sometimes assigned in modern
editions to Amiens the singer, who may have begun this song in which the
others join as they bear off the killer of the deer)   12 *burden* refrain

Enter Rosalind and Celia.   IV, iii

ROSALIND How say you now, is it not past two o'clock?
And here much Orlando!

CELIA I warrant you, with pure love and troubled brain,
he hath ta'en his bow and arrows and is gone forth to
sleep.
Enter Silvius.
Look who comes here.

SILVIUS
My errand is to you, fair youth.
My gentle Phebe did bid me give you this.
[Gives a letter.]
I know not the contents, but, as I guess
By the stern brow and waspish action
Which she did use as she was writing of it,
It bears an angry tenor. Pardon me;
I am but as a guiltless messenger.

ROSALIND
Patience herself would startle at this letter
And play the swaggerer. Bear this, bear all!
She says I am not fair, that I lack manners;
She calls me proud, and that she could not love me,
Were man as rare as phoenix. 'Od's my will!   18
Her love is not the hare that I do hunt.
Why writes she so to me? Well, shepherd, well,
This is a letter of your own device.

SILVIUS
No, I protest, I know not the contents.
Phebe did write it.

ROSALIND   Come, come, you are a fool,
And turned into the extremity of love.
I saw her hand. She has a leathern hand,
A freestone-colored hand. I verily did think   26
That her old gloves were on, but 'twas her hands.

IV, iii The Forest   **18** *phoenix* (there was supposed to be only one phoenix
in the world at a time)   **26** *freestone* soft sandstone or limestone, yellowish
brown

She has a housewife's hand ; but that's no matter :
I say she never did invent this letter ;
This is a man's invention and his hand.

SILVIUS
Sure it is hers.

ROSALIND
Why, 'tis a boisterous and a cruel style,
A style for challengers. Why, she defies me
Like Turk to Christian. Women's gentle brain
Could not drop forth such giant-rude invention,
Such Ethiop words, blacker in their effect
Than in their countenance. Will you hear the letter ?

SILVIUS
So please you, for I never heard it yet ;
Yet heard too much of Phebe's cruelty.

ROSALIND
40   She Phebes me. Mark how the tyrant writes.
(Read.) 'Art thou god, to shepherd turned,
           That a maiden's heart hath burned ?'
Can a woman rail thus ?

SILVIUS   Call you this railing ?

ROSALIND
45   *(Read.)* 'Why, thy godhead laid apart,
           Warr'st thou with a woman's heart ?'
Did you ever hear such railing ?
         'Whiles the eye of man did woo me,
49   That could do no vengeance to me.'
Meaning me a beast.
        'If the scorn of your bright eyne
         Have power to raise such love in mine,
         Alack, in me what strange effect
54   Would they work in mild aspect !
         Whiles you chid me, I did love ;
         How then might your prayers move !

---

40 *Phebes me* addresses me with her characteristic cruelty   45 *thy . . . apart*
i.e. as a god who has assumed human form   49 *vengeance* harm   54 *in mild
aspect* i.e. if they looked on me pleasantly

He that brings this love to thee
Little knows this love in me;
And by him seal up thy mind,   59
Whether that thy youth and kind   60
Will the faithful offer take
Of me and all that I can make,
Or else by him my love deny,
And then I'll study how to die.'

SILVIUS
Call you this chiding?
CELIA   Alas, poor shepherd!
ROSALIND Do you pity him? No, he deserves no pity.
Wilt thou love such a woman? What, to make thee an 68
instrument, and play false strains upon thee? Not to be
endured! Well, go your way to her, for I see love hath
made thee a tame snake, and say this to her: that if she 71
love me, I charge her to love thee; if she will not, I will
never have her unless thou entreat for her. If you be a
true lover, hence, and not a word; for here comes more
company.   *Exit Silvius.*
        Enter Oliver.

OLIVER
Good morrow, fair ones. Pray you, if you know,
Where in the purlieus of this forest stands   77
A sheepcote, fenced about with olive trees?
CELIA
West of this place, down in the neighbor bottom.   79
The rank of osiers by the murmuring stream   80
Left on your right hand brings you to the place.
But at this hour the house doth keep itself;
There's none within.

---

59 *seal ... mind* enclose your thoughts in a letter   60 *youth and kind* youthful
nature   68–69 *make ... upon thee* use you (with pun on *instrument*) and
deceive you at the same time   71 *snake* i.e. base creature   77 *in the purlieus*
within the borders   79 *neighbor bottom* nearby valley   80 *rank of osiers* row
of willows

OLIVER

If that an eye may profit by a tongue,
Then should I know you by description,
Such garments and such years : 'The boy is fair,
87 Of female favor, and bestows himself
88 Like a ripe sister ; the woman low,
And browner than her brother.' Are not you
The owner of the house I did enquire for ?

CELIA

It is no boast, being asked, to say we are.

OLIVER

Orlando doth commend him to you both,
And to that youth he calls his Rosalind
94 He sends this bloody napkin. Are you he ?

ROSALIND

I am. What must we understand by this ?

OLIVER

Some of my shame, if you will know of me
What man I am, and how and why and where
This handkercher was stained.

CELIA   I pray you tell it.

OLIVER

When last the young Orlando parted from you,
He left a promise to return again
Within a hour ; and pacing through the forest,
Chewing the food of sweet and bitter fancy,
Lo, what befell ! He threw his eye aside,
And mark what object did present itself :
Under an old oak, whose boughs were mossed with age
And high top bald with dry antiquity,
A wretched ragged man, o'ergrown with hair,
Lay sleeping on his back ; about his neck
A green and gilded snake had wreathed itself,
Who with her head, nimble in threats, approached
The opening of his mouth ; but suddenly,

87 *favor* features; *bestows* conducts   88 *ripe* mature   94 *napkin* handkerchief

Seeing Orlando, it unlinked itself
And with indented glides did slip away   113
Into a bush, under which bush's shade
A lioness, with udders all drawn dry,
Lay couching, head on ground, with catlike watch   116
When that the sleeping man should stir; for 'tis
The royal disposition of that beast
To prey on nothing that doth seem as dead.
This seen, Orlando did approach the man
And found it was his brother, his elder brother.

CELIA
O, I have heard him speak of that same brother,
And he did render him the most unnatural   123
That lived amongst men.

OLIVER   And well he might so do,
For well I know he was unnatural.

ROSALIND
But, to Orlando: did he leave him there,
Food to the sucked and hungry lioness?

OLIVER
Twice did he turn his back and purposed so;
But kindness, nobler ever than revenge,   129
And nature, stronger than his just occasion,
Made him give battle to the lioness,
Who quickly fell before him; in which hurtling   132
From miserable slumber I awaked.

CELIA
Are you his brother?

ROSALIND   Was it you he rescued?

CELIA
Was't you that did so oft contrive to kill him?

OLIVER
'Twas I. But 'tis not I. I do not shame
To tell you what I was, since my conversion
So sweetly tastes, being the thing I am.

113 *indented* sinuous   116 *couching* crouched   123 *render* describe   129
kindness affection in kinship   132 *hurtling* tumúlt

ROSALIND
But, for the bloody napkin?

139 **OLIVER**   By and by.
When from the first to last, betwixt us two,
141 Tears our recountments had most kindly bathed,
As how I came into that desert place:
In brief, he led me to the gentle Duke,
Who gave me fresh array and entertainment,
Committing me unto my brother's love,
Who led me instantly unto his cave,
There stripped himself, and here upon his arm
The lioness had torn some flesh away,
Which all this while had bled; and now he fainted,
And cried, in fainting, upon Rosalind.
151 Brief, I recovered him, bound up his wound;
And after some small space, being strong at heart,
He sent me hither, stranger as I am,
To tell this story, that you might excuse
His broken promise, and to give this napkin,
Dyed in his blood, unto the shepherd youth
That he in sport doth call his Rosalind.
[Rosalind swoons.]

CELIA
Why, how now, Ganymede, sweet Ganymede!

OLIVER
Many will swoon when they do look on blood.

CELIA
There is more in it. Cousin Ganymede!

OLIVER
Look, he recovers.

ROSALIND
I would I were at home.

CELIA   We'll lead you thither.
I pray you, will you take him by the arm?

139 *By and by* presently   141 *recountments* accounts (of events since we
separated)   151 *Brief* in brief; *recovered* revived

OLIVER Be of good cheer, youth. You a man! You lack a man's heart.

ROSALIND I do so, I confess it. Ah, sirrah, a body would think this was well counterfeited. I pray you tell your 167 brother how well I counterfeited. Heigh-ho!

OLIVER This was not counterfeit. There is too great testimony in your complexion that it was a passion of earnest. 170

ROSALIND Counterfeit, I assure you.

OLIVER Well then, take a good heart and counterfeit to be a man.

ROSALIND So I do; but, i' faith, I should have been a woman by right.

CELIA Come, you look paler and paler. Pray you draw homewards. Good sir, go with us.

OLIVER
That will I, for I must bear answer back
How you excuse my brother, Rosalind.

ROSALIND I shall devise something. But I pray you commend my counterfeiting to him. Will you go? *Exeunt.*

*

Enter [Touchstone the] Clown and Audrey. V, i

TOUCHSTONE We shall find a time, Audrey. Patience, gentle Audrey.

AUDREY Faith, the priest was good enough, for all the old gentleman's saying.

TOUCHSTONE A most wicked Sir Oliver, Audrey, a most vile Mar-text. But, Audrey, there is a youth here in the forest lays claim to you.

AUDREY Ay, I know who 'tis. He hath no interest in me in the world. Here comes the man you mean.
Enter William.

---

167 *counterfeited* acted, pretended 170 *passion of earnest* display of genuine emotion
V, i The Forest

10 TOUCHSTONE It is meat and drink to me to see a clown;
    by my troth, we that have good wits have much to
12   answer for. We shall be flouting; we cannot hold.

WILLIAM Good ev'n, Audrey.

AUDREY God ye good ev'n, William.

WILLIAM And good ev'n to you, sir.

TOUCHSTONE Good ev'n, gentle friend. Cover thy head,
    cover thy head. Nay, prithee be covered. How old are
    you, friend?

WILLIAM Five-and-twenty, sir.

TOUCHSTONE A ripe age. Is thy name William?

WILLIAM William, sir.

TOUCHSTONE A fair name. Wast born i' th' forest here?

WILLIAM Ay, sir, I thank God.

TOUCHSTONE 'Thank God.' A good answer. Art rich?

WILLIAM Fair, sir, so so.

TOUCHSTONE 'So so' is good, very good, very excellent
    good; and yet it is not, it is but so so. Art thou wise?

WILLIAM Ay, sir, I have a pretty wit.

29 TOUCHSTONE Why, thou say'st well. I do now remem-
    ber a saying, 'The fool doth think he is wise, but the
    wise man knows himself to be a fool.' The heathen
    philosopher, when he had a desire to eat a grape, would
    open his lips when he put it into his mouth, meaning
    thereby that grapes were made to eat and lips to open.
    You do love this maid?

WILLIAM I do, sir.

TOUCHSTONE Give me your hand. Art thou learned?

WILLIAM No, sir.

TOUCHSTONE Then learn this of me: to have is to have;
    for it is a figure in rhetoric that drink, being poured out
    of a cup into a glass, by filling the one doth empty the

---

10 *clown* yokel (with a play on Touchstone's own profession)   12 *flouting*
mocking; *hold* i.e. hold our tongues   29–34 *I do . . . to open* (in this and the
following passages Touchstone is burlesquing the style of Lyly's *Euphues*
and Lodge's *Rosalynde*)

other; for all your writers do consent that *ipse* is he. 42
Now, you are not *ipse*, for I am he.

WILLIAM Which he, sir?

TOUCHSTONE He, sir, that must marry this woman.
Therefore, you clown, abandon (which is in the vulgar,
leave) the society (which in the boorish is, company) of
this female (which in the common is, woman); which
together is, abandon the society of this female, or, clown,
thou perishest; or, to thy better understanding, diest;
or, to wit, I kill thee, make thee away, translate thy life
into death, thy liberty into bondage. I will deal in poison
with thee, or in bastinado, or in steel; I will bandy with 53
thee in faction; I will o'errun thee with policy; I will 54
kill thee a hundred and fifty ways. Therefore tremble
and depart.

AUDREY Do, good William.

WILLIAM God rest you, merry sir. *Exit.*
        Enter Corin.

CORIN Our master and mistress seeks you. Come away,
away!

TOUCHSTONE Trip, Audrey, trip, Audrey. I attend, I
attend. *Exeunt.*

*

Enter Orlando and Oliver. V, ii

ORLANDO Is't possible that on so little acquaintance you
should like her? that but seeing, you should love her?
and loving, woo? and wooing, she should grant? And
will you persever to enjoy her?

OLIVER Neither call the giddiness of it in question, the 5
poverty of her, the small acquaintance, my sudden wooing, nor her sudden consenting; but say with me, I love

42 *ipse is he* he is the man ('ipse' was a fashionable literary term; Touchstone
doubtless alludes to its use in *Euphues*) 53 *bastinado* beating with sticks
53–54 *bandy . . . faction* engage in controversy with you 54 *o'errun . . .
policy* overwhelm you with political cunning
V, ii The Forest 5 *Neither . . . question* do not raise questions about the
speed of it

Aliena; say with her that she loves me; consent with both that we may enjoy each other. It shall be to your good; for my father's house, and all the revenue that

11 was old Sir Rowland's, will I estate upon you, and here live and die a shepherd.

Enter Rosalind.

ORLANDO You have my consent. Let your wedding be to-morrow: thither will I invite the Duke and all 's contented followers. Go you and prepare Aliena; for look you, here comes my Rosalind.

ROSALIND God save you, brother.

18 OLIVER And you, fair sister.   *[Exit.]*

ROSALIND O my dear Orlando, how it grieves me to see thee wear thy heart in a scarf!

ORLANDO It is my arm.

ROSALIND I thought thy heart had been wounded with the claws of a lion.

ORLANDO Wounded it is, but with the eyes of a lady.

ROSALIND Did your brother tell you how I counterfeited

26 to sound when he showed me your handkercher?

ORLANDO Ay, and greater wonders than that.

ROSALIND O, I know where you are! Nay, 'tis true. There was never anything so sudden but the fight of two rams

30 and Caesar's thrasonical brag of 'I came, saw, and overcame'; for your brother and my sister no sooner met but they looked; no sooner looked but they loved; no sooner loved but they sighed; no sooner sighed but they asked one another the reason; no sooner knew the reason but

35 they sought the remedy: and in these degrees have they made a pair of stairs to marriage, which they will climb

37 incontinent, or else be incontinent before marriage:

11 *estate* settle   18 *fair sister* (although Rosalind is still dressed like a man, Oliver addresses her according to the manner in which she has been described to him by Orlando; see IV, iii, 86–88)   26 *to sound* swooning   30 *thrasonical* boastful (like the braggart soldier, Thraso, in Terence's comedy *Eunuchus*)   35 *degrees* (Rosalind puns on the literal meaning 'steps')   37 *incontinent . . . incontinent* immediately . . . unrestrained sexually

they are in the very wrath of love, and they will to- 38
gether; clubs cannot part them. 39

ORLANDO They shall be married to-morrow, and I will
bid the Duke to the nuptial. But, O, how bitter a thing it
is to look into happiness through another man's eyes!
By so much the more shall I to-morrow be at the height
of heart-heaviness, by how much I shall think my
brother happy in having what he wishes for.

ROSALIND Why then, to-morrow I cannot serve your
turn for Rosalind?

ORLANDO I can live no longer by thinking.

ROSALIND I will weary you then no longer with idle talking. Know of me then, for now I speak to some purpose,
that I know you are a gentleman of good conceit. I speak 51
not this that you should bear a good opinion of my knowledge, insomuch I say I know you are; neither do I labor
for a greater esteem than may in some little measure
draw a belief from you, to do yourself good, and not to 55
grace me. Believe then, if you please, that I can do 56
strange things. I have, since I was three years old, con- 57
versed with a magician, most profound in his art and yet
not damnable. If you do love Rosalind so near the heart 59
as your gesture cries it out, when your brother marries 60
Aliena shall you marry her. I know into what straits of
fortune she is driven; and it is not impossible to me, if it
appear not inconvenient to you, to set her before your 63
eyes to-morrow, human as she is, and without any
danger.

ORLANDO Speak'st thou in sober meanings?

ROSALIND By my life, I do, which I tender dearly, 67
though I say I am a magician. Therefore put you in your

---

38 *wrath* passion **39** *clubs* (commonly used to part combatants) **51**
conceit intelligence **55** *belief* i.e. confidence in my ability **56** *grace me*
bring favor on myself **57** *conversed* had dealings **59** *not damnable* not
practicing black magic **60** *gesture . . . out* behavior proclaims **63** *inconvenient* inappropriate **67** *tender* value (the practice of magic was a
capital offense. Rosalind is slyly admitting that she is not truly a magician.)

best array, bid your friends; for if you will be married
to-morrow, you shall; and to Rosalind, if you will.

Enter Silvius and Phebe.

Look, here comes a lover of mine and a lover of hers.

PHEBE
Youth, you have done me much ungentleness
To show the letter that I writ to you.

ROSALIND
74 I care not if I have. It is my study
To seem despiteful and ungentle to you.
You are there followed by a faithful shepherd:
Look upon him, love him; he worships you.

PHEBE
Good shepherd, tell this youth what 'tis to love.

SILVIUS
It is to be all made of sighs and tears;
And so am I for Phebe.

PHEBE And I for Ganymede.

ORLANDO And I for Rosalind.

ROSALIND And I for no woman.

SILVIUS
It is to be all made of faith and service;
And so am I for Phebe.

PHEBE And I for Ganymede.

ORLANDO And I for Rosalind.

ROSALIND And I for no woman.

SILVIUS
89 It is to be all made of fantasy,
All made of passion, and all made of wishes,
91 All adoration, duty, and observance,
All humbleness, all patience, and impatience,
93 All purity, all trial, all observance;
And so am I for Phebe.

PHEBE And so am I for Ganymede.

---

74 *study* conscious endeavor 89 *fantasy* fancy 91 *observance* devotion
93 *observance* (many editors, assuming a compositor's error from two lines
above, emend to 'obedience')

ORLANDO And so am I for Rosalind.

ROSALIND And so am I for no woman.

PHEBE *[to Rosalind]*
     If this be so, why blame you me to love you?

SILVIUS *[to Phebe]*
     If this be so, why blame you me to love you?

ORLANDO
     If this be so, why blame you me to love you?

ROSALIND Why do you speak too, 'Why blame you me 101
     to love you?'

ORLANDO
     To her that is not here, nor doth not hear.

ROSALIND Pray you, no more of this; 'tis like the howling 103
     of Irish wolves against the moon. *[to Silvius]* I will help
     you if I can. *[to Phebe]* I would love you if I could.
     To-morrow meet me all together. *[to Phebe]* I will
     marry you if ever I marry woman, and I'll be married
     to-morrow. *[to Orlando]* I will satisfy you if ever I satis-
     fied man, and you shall be married to-morrow. *[to
     Silvius]* I will content you if what pleases you contents
     you, and you shall be married to-morrow. *[to Orlando]*
     As you love Rosalind, meet. *[to Silvius]* As you love
     Phebe, meet. And as I love no woman, I'll meet. So
     fare you well. I have left you commands.

SILVIUS I'll not fail if I live.

PHEBE Nor I.

ORLANDO Nor I.   *Exeunt.*

                    *

     Enter [Touchstone the] Clown and Audrey.   V, iii

TOUCHSTONE To-morrow is the joyful day, Audrey; to-
     morrow will we be married.

AUDREY I do desire it with all my heart; and I hope it is

---

101 *Why . . . too* (often emended to 'Who . . . to') 103-04 *like . . . moon*
(corresponding simile in *Rosalynde* reads: 'thou barkest with the wolves of
Syria against the moon')
V, iii The Forest

4   no dishonest desire to desire to be a woman of the world.
Here come two of the banished Duke's pages.

Enter two Pages.

1 . PAGE Well met, honest gentleman.

TOUCHSTONE By my troth, well met. Come, sit, sit, and
a song!

9 2 . PAGE We are for you. Sit i' th' middle.

10 1 . PAGE Shall we clap into't roundly, without hawking or
11   spitting or saying we are hoarse, which are the only
prologues to a bad voice?

2 . PAGE I' faith, i' faith! and both in a tune, like two
gypsies on a horse.

Song.

It was a lover and his lass,
   With a hey, and a ho, and a hey nonino,
17 That o'er the green cornfield did pass
18   In springtime, the only pretty ringtime,
When birds do sing, hey ding a ding, ding.
Sweet lovers love the spring.

Between the acres of the rye,
   With a hey, and a ho, and a hey nonino,
These pretty country folks would lie
   In springtime, &c.

This carol they began that hour,
   With a hey, and a ho, and a hey nonino,
How that a life was but a flower
   In springtime, &c.

And therefore take the present time,
   With a hey, and a ho, and a hey nonino,
31 For love is crownèd with the prime
   In springtime, &c.

---

4 *dishonest* immodest; *to be . . . world* to be married (and also to go beyond
her present rustic station in life) 9 *for you* ready for you 10 *clap into't
roundly* start right off 11 *only* common 17 *cornfield* wheatfield 18
ringtime wedding season 31 *prime* spring

TOUCHSTONE Truly, young gentlemen, though there
   was no great matter in the ditty, yet the note was very un- 34
   tuneable.

1. PAGE You are deceived, sir. We kept time, we lost not
   our time.

TOUCHSTONE By my troth, yes; I count it but time lost
   to hear such a foolish song. God b' wi' you, and God
   mend your voices. Come, Audrey.   *Exeunt.*

                               *

   Enter Duke Senior, Amiens, Jaques, Orlando,   V, iv
   Oliver, Celia.

DUKE SENIOR
   Dost thou believe, Orlando, that the boy
   Can do all this that he hath promisèd?

ORLANDO
   I sometimes do believe, and sometimes do not,
   As those that fear they hope, and know they fear.   4
        Enter Rosalind, Silvius, and Phebe.

ROSALIND
   Patience once more, whiles our compact is urged.   5
   You say, if I bring in your Rosalind,
   You will bestow her on Orlando here?

DUKE SENIOR
   That would I, had I kingdoms to give with her.

ROSALIND
   And you say you will have her when I bring her?

ORLANDO
   That would I, were I of all kingdoms king.

ROSALIND
   You say you'll marry me, if I be willing?

PHEBE
   That will I, should I die the hour after.

---

34 *untuneable* untuneful
V, iv The Forest   4 *fear they hope* i.e. fear they only hope   5 *urged* stressed

ROSALIND
But if you do refuse to marry me,
You'll give yourself to this most faithful shepherd?

PHEBE
So is the bargain.

ROSALIND
You say that you'll have Phebe, if she will?

SILVIUS
Though to have her and death were both one thing.

ROSALIND
18 I have promised to make all this matter even.
Keep you your word, O Duke, to give your daughter;
You yours, Orlando, to receive his daughter;
Keep you your word, Phebe, that you'll marry me,
Or else, refusing me, to wed this shepherd;
Keep your word, Silvius, that you'll marry her
If she refuse me; and from hence I go,
25 To make these doubts all even.
                              Exeunt Rosalind and Celia.

DUKE SENIOR
I do remember in this shepherd boy
27 Some lively touches of my daughter's favor.

ORLANDO
My lord, the first time that I ever saw him
Methought he was a brother to your daughter.
But, my good lord, this boy is forest-born,
And hath been tutored in the rudiments
32 Of many desperate studies by his uncle,
Whom he reports to be a great magician,
34 Obscurèd in the circle of this forest.
                 Enter [Touchstone the] Clown and Audrey.

35 JAQUES There is, sure, another flood toward, and these

---

18 *even* plain   25 *make . . . even* clear up your misgivings   27 *lively* life-like; *favor* features   32 *desperate* dangerous   34 *Obscurèd* hidden   35 *toward* approaching   35–36 *these couples . . . ark* (see Genesis vii, 2, where only the 'unclean beasts' go into the ark by couples)

couples are coming to the ark. Here comes a pair of very strange beasts, which in all tongues are called fools.

TOUCHSTONE Salutation and greeting to you all!

JAQUES Good my lord, bid him welcome. This is the motley-minded gentleman that I have so often met in the forest. He hath been a courtier, he swears.

TOUCHSTONE If any man doubt that, let him put me to my purgation. I have trod a measure; I have flattered a 43 lady; I have been politic with my friend, smooth with 44 mine enemy; I have undone three tailors; I have had 45 four quarrels, and like to have fought one.

JAQUES And how was that ta'en up? 47

TOUCHSTONE Faith, we met, and found the quarrel was upon the seventh cause.

JAQUES How seventh cause? Good my lord, like this fellow.

DUKE SENIOR I like him very well.

TOUCHSTONE God 'ild you, sir; I desire you of the like. I 52 press in here, sir, amongst the rest of the country copu- 53 latives, to swear and to forswear, according as marriage binds and blood breaks. A poor virgin, sir, an ill-favored 55 thing, sir, but mine own; a poor humor of mine, sir, to 56 take that that no man else will. Rich honesty dwells like 57 a miser, sir, in a poor house, as your pearl in your foul oyster.

DUKE SENIOR By my faith, he is very swift and senten- 60 tious.

TOUCHSTONE According to the fool's bolt, sir, and such 62 dulcet diseases. 63

JAQUES But, for the seventh cause. How did you find the quarrel on the seventh cause?

---

43 *purgation* trial, proof; *measure* dance, with measured steps   44 *politic* prudent   45 *undone* ruined   47 *ta'en up* settled   52 *'ild* reward; *I desire ... like* I wish you the same compliment   53 *copulatives* i.e. those about to couple   55 *blood* passion   56 *humor* eccentricity   57 *honesty* chastity   60 *sententious* full of sense   62 *bolt* arrow (which is quickly shot)   63 *dulcet diseases* pleasant afflictions

TOUCHSTONE Upon a lie seven times removed (bear your
66 body more seeming, Audrey) as thus, sir. I did dislike
the cut of a certain courtier's beard. He sent me word,
if I said his beard was not cut well, he was in the mind
it was: this is called the Retort Courteous. If I sent him
word again it was not well cut, he would send me word
71 he cut it to please himself: this is called the Quip Modest.
72 If again, it was not well cut, he disabled my judgment:
this is called the Reply Churlish. If again, it was not well
cut, he would answer I spake not true: this is called the
Reproof Valiant. If again, it was not well cut, he would
76 say I lie: this is called the Countercheck Quarrelsome:
77 and so to the Lie Circumstantial and the Lie Direct.

JAQUES And how oft did you say his beard was not well
cut?

TOUCHSTONE I durst go no further than the Lie Circumstantial, nor he durst not give me the Lie Direct;
and so we measured swords and parted.

JAQUES Can you nominate in order now the degrees of
the lie?

85 TOUCHSTONE O sir, we quarrel in print, by the book, as
you have books for good manners. I will name you the
degrees. The first, the Retort Courteous; the second,
the Quip Modest; the third, the Reply Churlish; the
fourth, the Reproof Valiant; the fifth, the Countercheck
90 Quarrelsome; the sixth, the Lie with Circumstance; the
seventh, the Lie Direct. All these you may avoid but the
Lie Direct, and you may avoid that too, with an If. I
93 knew when seven justices could not take up a quarrel,
but when the parties were met themselves, one of them
thought but of an If: as, 'If you said so, then I said so';
and they shook hands and swore brothers. Your If is the

---

66 *seeming* properly   71 *Modest* moderate   72 *disabled* disqualified   76
Countercheck contradiction   77 *Circumstantial* indirect   85 *by the book*
according to the rules   90 *with Circumstance* i.e. only circumstantial,
indirect   93 *take up* settle

only peacemaker. Much virtue in If.

JAQUES Is not this a rare fellow, my lord? He's as good at
anything, and yet a fool.

DUKE SENIOR He uses his folly like a stalking horse, and 100
under the presentation of that he shoots his wit.   101

        Enter Hymen, Rosalind, and Celia. Still music.

HYMEN   Then is there mirth in heaven
             When earthly things made even
                 Atone together.   104
             Good Duke, receive thy daughter;
             Hymen from heaven brought her,
                 Yea, brought her hither,
             That thou mightst join her hand with his
             Whose heart within his bosom is.

ROSALIND *[to Duke]*
    To you I give myself, for I am yours.
        [To Orlando]
    To you I give myself, for I am yours.

DUKE SENIOR
    If there be truth in sight, you are my daughter.   112

ORLANDO
    If there be truth in sight, you are my Rosalind.

PHEBE
    If sight and shape be true,
    Why then, my love adieu!

ROSALIND *[to Duke]*
    I'll have no father, if you be not he.
        [To Orlando]
    I'll have no husband, if you be not he.
        [To Phebe]
    Nor ne'er wed woman, if you be not she.

---

100 *stalking horse* any object used to hide a hunter stalking game   101 *under
. . . that* i.e. while using the guise of his folly   s.d. *Hymen* the god of marriage (symbolizing, as in *The Two Noble Kinsmen*, a stage wedding); *Still*
soft   104 *Atone* are set at one, join   112 *If . . . sight* i.e. if he is not again
deceived by appearances

HYMEN   Peace ho! I bar confusion:
           'Tis I must make conclusion
              Of these most strange events.
           Here's eight that must take hands
           To join in Hymen's bands,
124   If truth holds true contents.
          [To Orlando and Rosalind]
125   You and you no cross shall part.
          [To Oliver and Celia]
           You and you are heart in heart.
          [To Phebe]
127   You to his love must accord,
           Or have a woman to your lord.
          [To Touchstone and Audrey]
129   You and you are sure together
           As the winter to foul weather.
          [To all]
           Whiles a wedlock hymn we sing,
132   Feed yourselves with questioning,
133   That reason wonder may diminish
           How thus we met, and these things finish.

Song.

    Wedding is great Juno's crown,
       O blessed bond of board and bed!
    'Tis Hymen peoples every town;
       High wedlock then be honorèd.
    Honor, high honor, and renown
    To Hymen, god of every town!

DUKE SENIOR
    O my dear niece, welcome thou art to me,
142   Even daughter, welcome, in no less degree!

124 *If . . . contents* i.e. if the discoveries made by the couples reveal their genuine affections   125 *cross* disagreement   127 *accord* assent   129 *sure together* securely united   132 *Feed* satisfy   133 *reason* understanding   142 *Even daughter* just as if you were my daughter

PHEBE *[to Silvius]*

    I will not eat my word, now thou art mine;   143

    Thy faith my fancy to thee doth combine.   144

        Enter Second Brother.

2. BROTHER

    Let me have audience for a word or two.

    I am the second son of old Sir Rowland

    That bring these tidings to this fair assembly.

    Duke Frederick, hearing how that every day

    Men of great worth resorted to this forest,

    Addressed a mighty power, which were on foot   150

    In his own conduct, purposely to take   151

    His brother here and put him to the sword;

    And to the skirts of this wild wood he came,

    Where, meeting with an old religious man,   154

    After some question with him, was converted   155

    Both from his enterprise and from the world,

    His crown bequeathing to his banished brother,

    And all their lands restored to them again

    That were with him exiled. This to be true

    I do engage my life.   160

DUKE SENIOR   Welcome, young man.

    Thou offer'st fairly to thy brothers' wedding: 161

    To one, his lands withheld; and to the other,

    A land itself at large, a potent dukedom.

    First, in this forest let us do those ends   164

    That here were well begun and well begot;

    And after, every of this happy number

    That have endured shrewd days and nights with us   167

    Shall share the good of our returnèd fortune,

    According to the measure of their states.   169

---

143 *eat* swallow, i.e. take back 144 *combine* unite s.d. *Second Brother* i.e. Jaques de Boys 150 *Addressed* assembled; *power* force (of troops) 151 *conduct* command 154 *religious man* (evidently an anchorite) 155 *question* discussion 160 *engage* pledge 161 *Thou . . . fairly* you bring handsome prospects 164 *do those ends* complete those purposes 167 *shrewd* sharp, hard 169 *states* i.e. status

Meantime forget this new-fall'n dignity
And fall into our rustic revelry.
Play, music, and you brides and bridegrooms all,
With measure heaped in joy, to th' measures fall.

JAQUES

Sir, by your patience. If I heard you rightly,
175   The Duke hath put on a religious life
And thrown into neglect the pompous court.

2. BROTHER   He hath.

JAQUES

178   To him will I. Out of these convertites
There is much matter to be heard and learned.
      [To Duke]
You to your former honor I bequeath ;
Your patience and your virtue well deserves it.
      [To Orlando]
You to a love that your true faith doth merit ;
      [To Oliver]
You to your land and love and great allies ;
      [To Silvius]
You to a long and well-deservèd bed ;
      [To Touchstone]
And you to wrangling, for thy loving voyage
Is but for two months victualled. So, to your pleasures :
I am for other than for dancing measures.

DUKE SENIOR   Stay, Jaques, stay.

JAQUES

To see no pastime I. What you would have
I'll stay to know at your abandoned cave.   *Exit.*

DUKE SENIOR

Proceed, proceed. We'll begin these rites,
As we do trust they'll end, in true delights.
                                    Exit [in the dance].

---

175 *put . . . life* adopted the life of a monk or hermit   178 *convertites*
converts

[EPILOGUE]

ROSALIND It is not the fashion to see the lady the epilogue, but it is no more unhandsome than to see the lord the 2 prologue. If it be true that good wine needs no bush, 'tis 3 true that a good play needs no epilogue; yet to good wine they do use good bushes, and good plays prove the better by the help of good epilogues. What a case am I 6 in then, that am neither a good epilogue, nor cannot insinuate with you in the behalf of a good play! I am 8 not furnished like a beggar; therefore to beg will not 9 become me. My way is to conjure you, and I'll begin 10 with the women. I charge you, O women, for the love you bear to men, to like as much of this play as please 12 you; and I charge you, O men, for the love you bear to women (as I perceive by your simp'ring none of you hates them), that between you and the women the play may please. If I were a woman, I would kiss as many 16 of you as had beards that pleased me, complexions that liked me, and breaths that I defied not; and I am sure, 18 as many as have good beards, or good faces, or sweet breaths, will, for my kind offer, when I make curtsy, bid 20 me farewell. *Exit.*

Epi. 2 *unhandsome* unbecoming 3 *bush* ivy bush (formerly the sign of a vintner) 6 *case* predicament 8 *insinuate* ingratiate myself 9 *furnished* equipped, i.e. with rags and cup 10 *conjure* adjure, i.e. charge, as if on oath 12 *like* (a reminder of the play's title); *please* may please 16 *If . . . woman* (a reminder that the actor was a boy) 18 *liked me* I liked; *defied* rejected 20–21 *bid me farewell* i.e. with applause

THREE COMEDIES

Ben Jonson
Edited by Michael Jamieson

As Shakespeare's nearest rival on the English stage, Ben Jonson has both gained and suffered. Productions of recent years have, as it were, rediscovered him as a comic dramatist of genius and a master of language. This volume contains his best-known comedies. *Volpone*, which is perhaps his greatest, and *The Alchemist* are both tours de force of brilliant knavery, unflagging in wit and comic invention. *Bartholomew Fair*, an earthier work, portrays Jonson's fellow Londoners in festive mood—bawdy, energetic, and never at a loss for words.

PENGUIN CLASSICS

The Penguin Classics, the earliest and most varied series of world masterpieces to be published in paperback, began in 1946 with E. V. Rieu's now famous translation of *The Odyssey*. Since then the series has commanded the unqualified respect of scholars and teachers throughout the English-speaking world. It now includes more than three hundred volumes, and the number increases yearly. In them, the great writings of all ages and civilizations are rendered into vivid, living English that captures both the spirit and the content of the original. Each volume begins with an introductory essay, and most contain notes, maps, glossaries, or other material to assist the reader in appreciating the work fully. Some volumes available include:

Aeschylus, THE ORESTEIAN TRILOGY
Honoré de Balzac, COUSIN BETTE
Geoffrey Chaucer, THE CANTERBURY TALES
Fyodor Dostoyevsky, THE BROTHERS KARAMAZOV
(2 volumes)
THE EPIC OF GILGAMESH
Gustave Flaubert, MADAME BOVARY
Nikolai Gogol, DEAD SOULS
Henrik Ibsen, HEDDA GABLER AND OTHER PLAYS
Friedrich Nietzsche, THUS SPOKE ZARATHUSTRA
Plato, THE LAST DAYS OF SOCRATES
Sophocles, THE THEBAN PLAYS
Stendhal, SCARLET AND BLACK
Leo Tolstoy, ANNA KARENIN
Ivan Turgenev, FATHERS AND SONS
Émile Zola, GERMINAL

THE PENGUIN ENGLISH LIBRARY

The Penguin English Library Series reproduces, in convenient but authoritative editions, many of the greatest classics in English literature from Elizabethan times through the nineteenth century. Each volume is introduced by a critical essay, enhancing the understanding and enjoyment of the work for the student and general reader alike. A few selections from the list of more than one hundred titles follow:

PERSUASION, *Jane Austen*

PRIDE AND PREJUDICE, *Jane Austen*

SENSE AND SENSIBILITY, *Jane Austen*

JANE EYRE, *Charlotte Brontë*

WUTHERING HEIGHTS, *Emily Brontë*

THE WAY OF ALL FLESH, *Samuel Butler*

THE WOMAN IN WHITE, *Wilkie Collins*

GREAT EXPECTATIONS, *Charles Dickens*

HARD TIMES, *Charles Dickens*

MIDDLEMARCH, *George Eliot*

TOM JONES, *Henry Fielding*

WIVES AND DAUGHTERS, *Elizabeth Gaskell*

MOBY DICK, *Herman Melville*

THE SCIENCE FICTION OF EDGAR ALLAN POE

VANITY FAIR, *William Makepeace Thackeray*

CAN YOU FORGIVE HER?, *Anthony Trollope*

PHINEAS FINN, *Anthony Trollope*

THE NATURAL HISTORY OF SELBORNE, *Gilbert White*

PLAYS BY BERNARD SHAW

ANDROCLES AND THE LION

THE APPLE CART

ARMS AND THE MAN

BACK TO METHUSELAH

CAESAR AND CLEOPATRA

CANDIDA

THE DEVIL'S DISCIPLE

THE DOCTOR'S DILEMMA

HEARTBREAK HOUSE

MAJOR BARBARA

MAN AND SUPERMAN

THE MILLIONAIRESS

PLAYS UNPLEASANT
(WIDOWERS' HOUSES, THE PHILANDERER,
MRS WARREN'S PROFESSION)

PYGMALION

SAINT JOAN

SELECTED ONE ACT PLAYS
(THE SHEWING-UP OF BLANCO POSNET,
HOW HE LIED TO HER HUSBAND, O'FLAHERTY V.C.,
THE INCA OF PERUSALEM, ANNAJANSKA, VILLAGE WOOING,
THE DARK LADY OF THE SONNETS, OVERRULED,
GREAT CATHERINE, AUGUSTUS DOES HIS BIT,
THE SIX OF CALAIS)